Living

By

Brenda Kennedy

LULU EDITION

LULU ISBN: 978-1-365-30996-0

Books One and Two end in Cliffhangers

The Forgotten Trilogy

Book Two

Dedicated to Diane B. Jones

We've joined forces as authors, but soon became friends. As you often remind me, it's a marathon, not a sprint. But may I ask, are we almost there yet?

TABLE OF CONTENTS

Cast of Characters

Ava Emerson: Heroine and lead character

Claire Richards: Ava's mom

Marshall Richards: Ava's dad

Connor Emerson: Ava's dead husband

Brett and Nichole Emerson: Connor's mom and dad

Chase Murphy: Connor's colleague and Ava's best male friend

Skylar Sperry: Ava's friend and business partner

Lorraine: Connor's paralegal

Skylar's mom and brother: Jessica and Mark

Xander Jamison: Ava's boyfriend, a famous author

Jami Alexander: Xander's pen name

Drew: Xander's identical twin brother

Daniel: Xander's dad

Rachael: Xander's mom

Wesley: Xander's editor and friend

Dr. Adams: Ava's doctor

Olivia: Battered woman

Olivia's twin daughters: Abigail and Emily

Luke Tanner: Man who helped Olivia

Chapter One: Devastating News

Ava

"Don't talk, Xander, it'll be okay." He looks around the ambulance watching the staff and then the monitors. Then he inspects his hand and follows the IV line leading from his hand to the I.V. pole. The bags of fluid are swinging from the bumpy ride and he closes his eyes. *Good, maybe he'll rest.*

When he opens his eyes again, I give him my strongest smile as I gently hold his left hand.

"Ava, there's something you need to know about me." *What could he have to tell me? He has seizures? He's epileptic?* "I was going to tell you, but I didn't know how."

He pauses and I say, "You had a seizure." *I'll say something to help reduce his anxiety.* "There are medications that you can take…."

"No, Ava. It's not just the seizures." I still, and my heart races. I wait for him to find the words he's searching for. "I'm sorry, I don't know how to say it."

I squeeze his hand again. "Just say it, Xander. It can't be as bad as you think."

"Ava." He clears his throat. "I have cancer."

What? Cancer? I'm a nurse, I know what cancer is, but can this be right? He seems healthy. He doesn't appear to be sick... well, not before yesterday. "Xander, are you sure?" *What a stupid thing to say. If someone has cancer, of course they're sure.* "You can beat this. There's chemo, and radiation, and…"

"It's too late for that." He watches me with sad eyes.

I squeeze his hand a little tighter. "Wh... what do you mean, 'It's too late for that?'" I stutter. *What I'm thinking can't be right. I need to hear him say it. I need him to clarify what he means. It's too late today or this week. What does he mean?*

He turns his head so he's facing me directly. I notice, for the first time, the dark circles under his eyes, his dry lips, and the worry lines at the outside corner of his eyes. "Ava, I'm dying."

I just look at him without saying a word. What can I say? My eyes fill with tears as the ambulance turns a sharp corner. He's dying. He's talking about death. It's permanent. What can I say to him? It'll be all right? Don't worry about it? It's nothing? NO! I can't say anything. There's nothing for me to say. I kneel down beside him and rest my head on his chest. It's not to comfort him; it's to comfort myself.

We have arrived at the hospital, I can only watch in disbelief as they wheel Xander through the double doors of the emergency room and into the treatment rooms. I walk to Admissions as I call Rachael using Xander's phone.

"Xander, how are you?"

"It's Ava, Mrs. Jamison."

"It's Xander, isn't it?"

"It is. He's had a seizure."

"Ava, we'll be there as soon as we can. I need to speak to a nurse or a doctor about Xander's medical condition."

"Okay, let me find you one. Hold on."

I search for a nurse and tell her Xander's mother is on the phone. I try to listen, but the nurse walks away from me.

With blurred vision, I watch as she writes things down at the Admissions counter. Suddenly I feel nauseated. I call Skylar from my cell phone to tell her what happened and to see if she can meet me at the hospital.

"Ava, I can't leave. Someone has to stay here," she says.

Shit, I forgot about that. "Can you call Steve and Lou Ann? Maybe one of them would come over?"

"I'll see what I can do. I'll call you back."

"Thank you."

I wait in the E.R. by myself for what feels like hours before I see anyone. The nurses and the doctors won't let me go back with Xander until he's stabilized. They come out often, wanting to see if Xander's family has arrived. They haven't. I wait and pace. Staring at the clock, I wonder what is taking so long. Where's Skylar? She hasn't called or texted me. *Cancer? Can that be right? Maybe the medication they gave him to stop his seizures in the ambulance confused him?*

Skylar finally arrives after an hour and I cry. I cry over what I witnessed with Xander, I cry because he's in the emergency room alone, and I cry because he's dying of cancer. I don't love him, but I do like him. I don't want him to die; I don't want anyone to die.

"Skylar, he said he's dying of cancer!"

"Ava, are you sure that's what he said?"

I look at her straight in the eyes. "That's exactly what he said."

"I'm sorry, Ava. He just looks so healthy. Maybe he was confused."

That's exactly what I thought. "Maybe."

The entrance door to the emergency room opens and in walks two men with Xander's mom, Rachael.

"Ava, how is he?" She hugs me. Her eyes are red and swollen.

I didn't expect to see them here until the morning. "I don't know, I haven't seen him. They're waiting for you to get here."

"Ava and Skylar, this is Xander's father, Daniel, and his brother, Drew."

"It's nice to meet you," Skylar says. "How did you get here so fast?"

Drew says, "We flew in on our plane. It took a little longer than I expected because we ran into some unexpected turbulence."

Xander's twin brother has his pilot's license? It dawns on me how little I know about Xander and his family. "I'm glad you're here. We were at a festival and Xander had a seizure. I couldn't stop them." I cry and try to calm my nerves.

"I'll let the nurse know we're here." I watch as Daniel walks out of the room.

"Let's all sit down," Drew says.

Daniel returns and we wait briefly before the doctor calls his family back into the exam room. Skylar and I wait.

"Should I go back to the inn?" Skylar asks.

I look dismally at Skylar. "Would you wait just a little while longer?"

"Sure."

We both sit back and I try to relax. When it's useless I pace, make coffee, and straighten up the magazines before deciding I need to know something. I need to see Xander.

"Skylar, go home. I think I'll be here longer than I thought."

"Ava, I hate to leave you here alone."

"There's nothing you can do. I'll be home as soon as I see him. I just need to make sure he'll be all right." *At least for tonight.*

She looks at the double doors. "Okay, call me as soon as you hear something. I'll be back to get you when you're ready."

"What about the inn?"

"I think I can leave it unattended for half an hour or so."

"Okay, thank you for everything."

Skylar leaves and I wait. It isn't until the early morning hours that Xander's family walks out of the treatment room. They all look sad and broken. My heart stops. *Did he die?* I stand and wait for someone to say something... anything.

Rachael walks over and holds both of my hands. Her husband and son stand close. She looks devastated. Her face is blotchy and stained with tears. She looks older than her years. "Xander wants to see you, but they're moving him to a room first."

Thank God, he didn't die. I want to ask whether he has cancer, but I can't. I can't say the words out loud. Not yet. Not today. "How is he?"

Rachael says, "He's stable."

She offers no other information about Xander or his condition. I want to ask questions. I want to know what's wrong with him. I want to know whether he has terminal cancer.

"Let's go up to the third floor and wait for him, shall we?" Daniel says.

We wait for the elevator. The sign on the wall says, "Oncology, third floor." I don't think my legs will hold the weight of my body. Oh my God, Xander really has cancer? This can't be right. He looks fine. He doesn't look like the pictures of cancer patients I've seen in magazines or on television. I look at Daniel and he steps into the waiting elevator. I follow. The area is small, too small, and I feel like I'll suffocate if I don't get out. He pushes the third floor button. *Oncology.* Thankfully, the ride to the third floor doesn't take long. The silence of Xander's family is deafening. I look at Rachael, her lip quivers. I watch as a single tear trickles down her red cheek in slow motion. Daniel holds his wife tightly in his strong arms. Then, my eyes slowly drift to Drew. He looks so much like his brother. Dark hair, long thick eyelashes, strong jawline, tall, and very handsome. They look alike, almost identical, but I could tell them apart if they were standing side by side. It makes me sad that his brother Xander isn't here. I remember Xander telling me they used to break up with each other's girlfriends. How did those girls not know who was who? Xander's nose is thinner and more pinched at the bridge, his cheekbones are slightly higher, and he has a slight dimple in his chin. If Drew walked into a room, I would know right away he wasn't my boyfriend. *Boyfriend? Is Xander my boyfriend?*

"Ava, you can see him now," Drew says.

Drew is standing in front of me, and there's a nurse standing in the doorway so we walk in her direction. I feel like I'm entering the depths of hell. I feel like I'm going to see a sign that says, "ABANDON ALL HOPE, YE WHO ENTER HERE." I have this feeling of doom weighing heavy on me. I want to see him, but then I don't. He'll only confirm my worst fears.

I slowly walk off the elevator and walk behind the nurse with Drew by my side. When she stops at the closed door, she says, "He's expecting you."

"I'll wait for you here." I look at Drew and he looks defeated. *His twin brother is dying of cancer.*

"It's okay, Drew. I'll be okay." *He shouldn't be worried about me.*

He nods and walks away.

I walk cautiously into the room where Xander is in the hospital bed, wearing an old faded hospital gown. He doesn't look any different than he did yesterday. He is just as handsome as he was before the seizure. Maybe my fears are misplaced. Maybe he just had one seizure and he's on the Oncology unit because the hospital is full. *It could be an overflow unit, couldn't it? Maybe the meds they gave him confused him.*

"It looks like I owe you another date. I think I messed this one up, didn't I?"

I feel like a weight has been lifted from my shoulders. Xander is sitting up and speaking lightly about the seizure.

I ask cautiously, "How are you?" It's too soon for me to joke about his seizure. I may never be able to speak lightly about something so frightening.

"I'm better. I'm sorry you had to witness that." He holds my hand and strokes my knuckles.

"I wish I could have done something for you." *It was probably one of the scariest moments in my life.*

"From what I understand, everything you did helped me. Thank you."

I search his eyes. I need to see the truth when I ask the question that haunts me. "Are you going to be all right?" *I really want to ask, "Are you really dying?" but I can't say those words.*

He looks away from me and says, "I think I told you in the ambulance, I have cancer."

"You did. I was hoping it wasn't true." My stomach knots up in a ball. "How long have you been sick?"

He licks his dry lips. "A couple years."

My eyes get watery. "What kind of cancer do you have?"

He pauses before answering "I have brain cancer."

My heart breaks at the thought. "What stage is it?"

He swallows hard. "It's in the end stage."

Never taking my eyes off of his, I have to ask, "How long do you have?"

"A few months, maybe a year if I'm lucky."

"What about chemo or radiation?"

"I've done both."

"And surgery?"

"Ava?"

"Xander, I have to know."

"Where the tumor is located in my brain, it's not worth the risk."

A tear slides down my face. I'm going to lose him; just like Connor, I'm going to lose Xander.

"Don't cry."

I can't say anything. My mind won't accept the news.

"Come here." He pulls me lightly by the hand, and I lean in and hug him. He whispers into my ear. "My only regret is, I won't have more time with you."

I cry. His words are the sweetest I've ever heard. "Don't say that. We'll beat this. We'll find a way."

When the doctor assures us that Xander is stable, we leave. I call Skylar and ask her if there's an extra room at the inn and there is. I tell Daniel where Xander's car is parked and we drive over to get it so it won't be towed. I decide to ride home with Drew in Xander's car, and Daniel and Rachael follow us to the inn in their rental car.

Drew says, "You know, Xander's a very private person."

"I'm learning that." *Must be why he never told me about the cancer.*

"He was hoping he would never have to disclose his cancer to you, that you would never need to find out about it."

Thinking of Xander dying and me never knowing about it hurts. A tear falls and I wipe it away.

"Why is he here in Savannah, and not with his family?"

Drew watches the road. "When he got the news that the cancer was growing, he left. He said he needed time to let it sink in, to figure it out."

"He told me he was here to write a book."

"If he told you that, then he probably is. Xander does his best thinking while writing; he also does his best work under stress."

"Yeah, I can't think of anything more stressful." *Dying of cancer, is there anything more stressful?*

When we get to the inn, I show Drew Xander's room where he'll be staying, and I also show Daniel and Rachael their room. When they are all settled into their rooms, Skylar and I lock up.

Skylar says, "I called your mom. I figured we might need help with the inn while Xander's in the hospital. I figured you'd want to spend some time with him."

"Good, I'm glad you did. Is she coming to help out?" I don't ask about my dad. I know he has work and couldn't help out even if he wanted to.

"She'll be here sometime tomorrow."

"Sounds good."

"So, does he have cancer?" she asks.

"He does. It's just so hard to believe." I think about the night. "We went on a date and I never imagined it would end like this."

"How could you? It's hard to believe."

"It is. I'm exhausted and headed to bed. Goodnight, Skylar."

"Goodnight, Ava."

I shower, hoping to wash the news of the day off, but of course, it doesn't work. I lie in bed, unable to sleep. I can't get this nightmare out of my mind. It's hard to believe that this man, whom I like so much, is dying. He has only one year to live at the most. I cry myself to sleep.

I reluctantly get out of bed the next morning. I pray Xander's cancer was a nightmare and not a reality. I shower and start the day with much less enthusiasm than I usually have. Skylar also looks somber. We set the breakfast up for our guests as we normally do, but today, we forget the creamers for the coffee, and the first batch of biscuits burned. I try hard to focus on the inn, but my mind is at the hospital with Xander.

At breakfast, I learn that Xander's mom and dad have already left for the hospital. His brother Drew joins us for a quiet meal. When Skylar realizes that I am silent, she engages in conversations around the breakfast table.

"How long have you been flying?" she asks Drew.

"Just a couple years. I don't fly that far, just mostly along the East Coast, and it's mostly for sport."

"Does Xander fly, too?"

When I hear Xander's name, I pay more attention.

"No, he was always more interested in boating. Mom always joked about buying him a houseboat, because he spent so much time on the water."

I look at Drew; he reminds me of Xander. At breakfast, Drew stays until the last guest leaves. I thought Xander always stayed until the last guest left because he was interested in me, but maybe he did it because it's the polite thing to do. Or maybe Drew's interested in Skylar. When the last guest leaves, Drew says he's heading to the hospital.

Skylar also stands and says, "We packed some food for you guys to eat while you're there, and there's also some soup for Xander, if he's hungry."

"Thank you both; that is very kind of you."

"It's okay," Skylar says, handing him one of the smaller picnic baskets. "We wanted to do something, but weren't sure what to do."

"Sadly, there isn't anything anyone can do. This is nice and it's definitely appreciated. Thank you both again."

"Please tell Xander I'll be up later this evening. I have the inn to attend to, then we have an afternoon tea we need to set up for." I'm rambling and I don't know why. I think I want Drew to know I would be at the hospital if I could. I have obligations and I can't just get up and leave.

"I will, Ava. I know you both are busy here. Skylar, will you be coming with her?"

I look at Drew and then at Skylar. She smiles and says, "It depends if someone's here to watch the inn."

"Okay. Maybe I'll see you both later today."

He leaves and we clean up and get ready for the afternoon tea. I stay busy to keep my mind off of Xander. I get a text from an unknown number.

Unknown number: *Is my room ready? I'm coming home.*

Ava: *It all depends on who this is.*

Unknown number: *Sorry, using Drew's phone. It's Xander. I'm being released.*

My hearts beats a little too fast with excitement.

Ava: *The doctor is releasing you?*

Unknown number: *No, I'm leaving against medical advice.*

Is he serious? His mother wouldn't stand by and let him do that. But, could she really stop him?

Ava: *In that case, no. All of the rooms in this inn are sold out.*

Unknown number: *I'm kidding. My seizures are under control and as soon as I finish my soup, I'll be heading home to the inn, if that's all right with you.*

Why wouldn't it be all right with me? I'm just glad he's well enough to come home.

Ava: *In that case, your room is waiting for you with clean sheets and a mint on the pillow.*

Unknown number: *Good, I can't wait to see you. I missed you at breakfast this morning.*

That makes me smile.

Ava: *Me, too. Breakfast wasn't the same without you. I'll see you soon.*

I tell Skylar about Xander being released. She suggests we move him into a room with two double beds since his brother's here. They can share a room and we can free up a guest room for other guests. So we do that. I have no idea how long his family is staying, but it'll be nice for them while they're here. "That's a great idea. I'll call and make sure it's okay with Xander," I say. He's still a guest and I don't feel right just moving his things without his permission. Once I get the okay from Xander and his brother, I make sure the cleaners disinfect Xander's room better than usual. I'll do my part to keep him as healthy as I can, for as long as I can.

Mom shows up during the tea. I hug her and say, "Thank you for coming on such short notice."

"No thanks needed. I'm glad to be able to help out."

When the tea is over, we talk and I fill her in on the news about Xander. Mom met Xander briefly and she liked him. She doesn't know that we've grown closer since she's left. Mom makes a big pot of pasta with homemade spaghetti sauce for dinner, while Skylar and I make the salad.

When Xander and his family arrive, I greet them on the porch, while everyone else waits in the foyer. He looks better than he did last night. I tell them my Mom has made dinner for everyone. We gather around the large table in the kitchen, and Xander holds my hand secretly beneath the table. No one talks about cancer, or dying, or seizures. I can see Rachael relaxing when she realizes that Xander isn't the main topic at dinner. Everyone seems to get along; it's just one big family having a delicious meal. Rachael doesn't need to be reminded of Xander's illness, although she probably can't think of anything else.

After dinner I make sure that Xander is comfortable and has everything he needs in his room. Skylar even put a few bottles of water on his nightstand. I saw Drew walking outside with Skylar a few moments ago, so I thought this would be a good time to check on Xander. He's lying on the bed when I knock on his opened door.

"I was hoping I'd see you again this evening," he says, sitting up slightly in his bed.

"Just popping in to make sure you have everything."

"I have everything I need right here. I'd like to talk to you if you have a few minutes."

Not sure if I should sit on the bed or on the desk chair, I opt for the bed when he scoots over, making room for me. He takes my small hand in his. "I'm sorry about last night." He stops as if searching for the right words. "My plan was to stay at the inn and do some writing while I figured out what to do about the news I received about my cancer growing." He watches me. "I didn't expect to be so smitten with you." A smile crosses my lips because of his word choice — it's easy to tell he's a writer. "I wanted the cancer to be gone, so I could maybe begin a relationship with you. You are everything I never had, and everything I wanted." He stops and then says, "I didn't tell you in the beginning because there was no need to. I was here for a few weeks, then I would return home, and you would never see me again."

"I understand. I'm not upset you didn't tell me, I get it. I was just so scared last night."

"I'm sorry you had to witness that and go through it."

"It's okay. I'm just relieved you're here with me now."

"But when my feelings changed, I *couldn't* tell you. I couldn't find the right words. How do you tell someone you have terminal cancer?" He pauses and says, "I'm not sure where we go from here."

The phrase "terminal cancer" hurts my heart. I hate cancer and what it does to people. I like him, and I still like him even with the cancer. "Let's just take it one day at a time."

"I can do that."

"Good, so can I."

Xander

I kiss Ava sweetly on the lips before she leaves. I was happy and excited when she let me. I know that cancer isn't a communicable disease, but I still feared that it would frighten her. No one wants cancer, but I'm glad she isn't afraid of catching it from me. It sounds stupid, but many people are afraid of being around someone with it. It's not like the cold or the flu where it's easily spread from one person to the next, and I'm glad Ava is educated enough to know that.

Having cancer sucks, and yet many people in the Western world will die from it. In the United States, the top three causes of death in every state are cancer, stroke, and heart disease. Doing such things as exercising, eating health-promoting foods such as fruits and veggies, and not smoking can prevent many deaths from these causes, but genetics plays a role that we cannot control, and the older we get the more likely it becomes that we will have cancer, a stroke, and/or heart disease.

One reason for coming to Savannah was to write a book. Now that I've met Ava, I've made it my mission to finish this book before I die. *Lost in Savannah*, I hope, will be my best book ever. I'm thankful that I'm still well enough to write. I'm also grateful this book is already in my head, and I just have to put it to paper, or computer screen.

When the doctor told me my cancer is terminal, I asked how long I had left. Doctors tend to reply in percentages. He told me, "You have a 90 percent of being dead in 12 months." I estimated how many pages I can write comfortably in a month, and I figure that I can write 30 pages per month, but cancer can sap energy as it progresses, so I probably won't write any pages the last month or two. Therefore, I can probably write 300 pages. That's enough for what I want to do. Look at the Australian critic and author Clive James. Even while dying of leukemia, he produced books as if he were a printing press. He must not have had a girl like Ava.

My mother is worried about me, as is my father and my brother. I'm fine. I feel fine. They hover over me, making sure my meds are taken on time and around the clock. I know the cancer is growing, but I don't feel as though I'm going to die today, this week, or even this month. I want to finish this book, and then spend as much time with my family and Ava as I can.

I'm single, and I don't date often, because no one has caught or held my attention for long. Until I met Ava, I never imagined that when I decided to come to Savannah I would meet someone who would consume my every waking thought.

When I'm not surrounded by family, I'm writing. I'm thankful I'm a fast typist. I stay up late and get up early to ensure I get this book done before it's too late. This book just recently became a priority. My brother and I are sharing a room and he gets me. He understands my urgency, although he may not agree with it. Once they read it, they'll understand.

I was able to talk my dad into returning home, but Mom and Drew refused to leave with him. Ava and Skylar said they had vacancies so that wasn't an issue. Drew spends his time with Skylar, which allows me time to write. Mom stays in her room, so she is close enough to me in case I need her. Having rooms side by side could have its benefits.

My routine prior to the seizures has remained the same. I shower before dawn, and I'm the first one down for breakfast, so I can claim the seat closest to Ava. I wander around the gardens, and often write under the mossy oak trees. With the weather changing, the cold air seems to keep Ava and Skylar in the house more often in their downtime. I miss having Ava join me in the late afternoon when the inn finally calms down. We live in the South and the seasons often come later than in the North. For instance, for Halloween, we were still wearing shorts.

While Mom is in the tearoom having tea with another woman staying at the inn, I ask Drew, "Hey, come to the store with me, will ya?"

"You feeling okay?"

"I'm fine. I want to get something, but I need your help."

"Sure, tell Mom we're leaving, and I'll get the car keys."

When we pull into Home Depot, Drew jokes, "Are you planning on doing some remodeling?"

As I get out of the truck, I say, "Remodeling? No, I have a much better idea. Come on, I'll show you."

Once inside, he follows me to the outdoor and holiday section of the store. "Man, you want to get a Christmas tree?"

He's an idiot! I'm not even going to waste my time answering him. I continue to walk to the area I need. "I was thinking of getting one of these." I look at the different sizes and models of outdoor fireplaces.

"A wood-burning fireplace, nice," Drew says.

"Wood-burning or gas?" I ask.

"Wood-burning, for sure."

"We'll need wood, and not that expensive stuff they sell here. We'll need a small truckload or so."

"I saw an old tree in back of the inn. We could put that to good use."

"Good, you get permission to cut the tree down for firewood, while I put this together."

He laughs. "Yeah, that sounds fair. Since it'll be dark soon, I'll collect what firewood I can today and get permission to cut the tree down at a later date."

When we return to the inn, we unload the large box in the backyard, and Drew heads out to collect some firewood from the field out back.

Ava taps on the window and waves to me from inside the house. I wave back, forcing myself to get back to the job at hand. I would love to go into the house and spend some time with her. The more I talk to her, the more I like her. When I look back at the window, she's gone. She opens the door and yells, "Are we having a fire later?"

"I thought we would. Is that all right?" I tighten the screw.

"It's a great idea. I think it's a perfect night for it."

"Good, Drew's searching for firewood, now."

"If he knows what he's doing, tell him to cut that dead tree down out back."

I laugh and say, "If he knows what he's doing?"

She also laughs. "I didn't mean it like that. I just don't want him to get hurt."

"It's okay. I thought it was funny. As long as he doesn't have to climb the tree, he'll be able to figure it out."

Mom comes outside with a bottle of water and my afternoon meds. I take them like they'll help me. They won't; it's too late for that. I don't tell her. She doesn't want to hear it. We talk a few minutes before she leaves to find Drew.

Just as I'm finished with the fireplace, Ava comes outside carrying a tray. She smiles and I can't help but stare at her natural beauty. She's wearing jeans, work boots, and a red and black flannel shirt.

"Hey," she says as she gets closer to me.

"Hey, yourself." I stand and greet her.

"Where did your mom go? I just saw her out here."

"She went to find Drew." When I hear the screen door open again, I see Skylar walking outside. "What's going on?"

Ava kisses me and I take the tray from her and set it on the table beside me. "We thought we could have s'mores and hot chocolate outside tonight."

Skylar looks around and says. "All we need is some firewood."

"Wood? Did someone say something about wood?" I watch as Drew comes from behind the fence with a wheelbarrow full of firewood. Mom is walking beside him.

"Do you at least have the fireplace put together?" he asks as he makes his way closer to us.

I get dizzy, but I blink it away. Slowly sitting down, I don't falter with my words. "I do." Slowly I say, "Is that all the wood you managed to get?" I am teasing him.

"Nope, but it is all the wood I could carry this trip."

"Yay, I'll start the fire," Skylar says excitedly.

Ava sits beside me and holds my hand. "Sounds like a great idea to me."

"Me, too," I agree.

Once the fireplace is lit, Ava passes out the mugs of hot cocoa to everyone. I teasingly say, "I bet this isn't as good as Mom's hot cocoa."

"Excuse me?" she says, grinning.

I laugh, suddenly feeling embarrassed. "Mom makes it from scratch with heavy cream and chocolate chips. I'm sure yours is good…"

"But Mom's is better," Drew also teases.

Ava looks up at Skylar and then at Mom. They are both laughing. "Well, Mr. Xander Jamison. Would you like to wager a little something on this?"

Do I want to wager something on this? "Sure, A movie and a beer?" *Seems like a safe bet to me.*

She smirks, "Let's up the ante." *To what? I thought dinner and a beer was a safe bet.* My dick twitches at the thought. *Down, boy!* "How about dinner and a bottle of wine?"

I should have known. I lift my mug of cocoa. "If this is as good as Mom's homemade cocoa, I owe you dinner and a bottle of wine." I take a sip and then another sip. "I stand corrected. This is every bit as good as Mom's hot cocoa."

"In fact," Drew says, "it tastes just like Mom's."

I take another drink, a bigger drink this time, burning the roof of my mouth. I look at Ava, Skylar, and then Mom. They are all laughing. "You made this?" I say, pointing at Mom.

"You don't believe that I made it, Xander?" Ava places her hand over her heart as if she's pained from my lack of trust.

I'm not sure. I retaste it while I watch my mother. She'll never lie and if she is being the slightest dishonest, I can tell, we all can tell. Slowly I look at Ava. "No, I believe you made it with Mom's recipe."

Everyone laughs and Mom excuses herself to turn in for the night.

"Run while you can," I joke.

"I'll see everyone in the morning." She hugs everyone before leaving. Drew walks her into the house and returns with two throw blankets for the girls. We roast marshmallows in the fire, eat s'mores, and share childhood stories. Everyone has a story to tell but Ava. Skylar includes Ava when telling something from her childhood. If Drew noticed, he doesn't say anything. *Knowing my brother, he noticed. He's very observant.*

Drew tells a story of when he was in Boy Scouts, and stole a bucket of popcorn he was supposed to be selling. Mom and Dad were so mad, they made him work the money off by volunteering at the animal shelter every Saturday for a month.

He laughs now at the story, but I remember he was crying like a baby at the time he had to clean the kennels of waste.

"I was in Girl Scouts when I was younger," Skylar says. "You know those yummy cookies they sell every year?"

I snuggle closer to Ava. Drew says, "The Thin Mints, the Tagalongs, or the Trefoils?"

"Yeah, those ones, among others."

"Never heard of them," he says, laughing.

She rolls her eyes and it makes us laugh. "Ava and I were sitting at a booth outside of Walmart and I ate the entire box of cookies by myself."

"I bet your mom didn't make you work at the animal shelter," Drew says.

"No, she didn't. I was so sick that I had to go home, and I missed out on the ice cream party they had for the girls who sold the cookies."

Drew laughs as he watches Skylar. "That's almost as bad as cleaning shitty dog kennels."

She laughs and leans into him.

"What about you, Xander?" Skylar asks.

I notice for the first time at how close she and Drew are sitting. They aren't touching, but they're pretty close. "I was in the house reading, while Drew was out getting into trouble."

"Were you in Boy Scouts, too?" Ava asks.

"Drew and I were in everything together. Mom and Dad raised us as if we were conjoined twins." I laugh. "We dressed alike, we played the same sports, and we were even in the same classes together."

"Yeah, I think that lasted until middle school."

"I think you're right." I wrap my arm around Ava.

"Twins dressing alike in middle school might be social suicide," Skylar says seriously.

"Do ya think?" Drew teases. "If I hadn't put a stop to it, my brother would still be trying to look, dress, and act like me."

"Me? Dream on, brother. It's you who tried to be me."

Ava shivers and I say, "I need to get some work done before it gets too late. Are you guys coming?"

Ava stands and Skylar says, "We'll be in, in a few."

"Okay, good night," Ava says.

Ava walks me to my room and I kiss her goodnight.

Skylar

I watch as Ava and Xander walk into the house, and for the first time, I notice how unsteady he is on his feet.

"He's not doing so well," Drew says.

"Maybe he's just tired. I didn't notice it earlier today."

"Maybe."

"I know Ava said his cancer is terminal, but are you sure there isn't something anyone can do?"

"There's brain surgery, but it's risky. He'll die without it, and more than likely he'll die with it. He has a pretty grim prognosis."

"He doesn't want to take a chance that the surgery might work?"

"No. Where the tumor is, there's a slim chance for them to remove the whole tumor without causing permanent or serious injury to him. He'd rather die than live and be paralyzed or brain dead."

"I'm sorry."

"Thanks, Skylar. So am I."

Over the next few days, Xander, Drew, and Rachael spend a lot of time together. When Rachael rests, Drew and Xander spend time with Ava and me. I know that Xander gets up early and stays up late. Ava says he wants to finish his book while he can. If I was dying, the last thing I would want to do is to write a book. I'd spend my last days surrounded by my family, friends, and good food. I've been dieting for what feels like my entire adult life, so I would indulge in all the foods I've avoided over my lifetime. I say that now, but I probably wouldn't. I'd hope I would be among the small percent of people to survive terminal cancer and live to talk about it. I'd do everything I could to be in remission, no matter how slim the chance. But I would indulge in the healthy food I like. I would eat pints of blueberries and strawberries every day.

Thanksgiving is Thursday and Rachael and Claire decided we should decorate and have a Thanksgiving Day feast at the inn. Of course, Ava called Steve and Lou Ann to see what they do for the holidays. Not surprising to learn, they also cook for their guests because their family comes in for the weekend and so they make dinner for everyone. Lou Ann said that they have only a few guests who stay over the winter holidays. "We are usually busy for a week just before Christmas, but nothing to speak of the other days in December."

I'm not sure what got into Ava, but she goes outside in the garage, and starts to bring in the Christmas tree and the holiday decorations from storage.

"I thought Claire and Rachael said we should put up Thanksgiving decorations. Did they?"

Ava smiles while opening up several of the boxes. "They did. I thought it'd be nice to get the inn ready for Christmas while we're at it."

"Rushing the holidays a bit, aren't you?"

"Maybe a little." She looks up at me with sad puppy dog eyes. "I want Xander to have a nice holiday. Would you mind helping?"

I look at all of the clear totes sitting in the middle of the room. "Give me one of those C.D.'s, I need some Christmas music to get me in the mood."

Before the end of the day, every guest staying at the inn is helping to put up the decorations. When we run out of exterior lights, Drew and Xander leave to get some more. Rachael and Claire are very precise in telling them what kind of lights and decorations to buy. Apparently, you need candles, lots and lots of red and white candles, and cranberry-scented wax for the wax warmers. While the guys are gone, we continue to decorate the trees in the foyer to greet our guests, and we put the other one tree in the tearoom.

Claire and Rachael are getting close and it's nice to see them happy. Xander hasn't had any more problems with seizures, and it's a relief for everyone. I can see him grow weaker with every day that passes, but I don't mention it. He smiles, writes, and spends his spare time with Ava and his family. She likes him and if she's happy, that's all I care about. I do worry about her when... well, I just worry about her.

When Drew isn't with Rachael or Xander, he's with me. Like me, he loves the water and the beach. One day when I was headed down to Tybee Island, he kind of invited himself, and he's been going with me everyday since then. He's good company and I like being around him.

On Wednesday, Lou Ann came over to bake pies and desserts with us for Thanksgiving, while Steve stayed behind and entertained their family and guests. Daniel flew his plane in to spend the holidays with his family at the inn. Marshall called and said he couldn't come; the only thing I could make out between Claire's sobs is something about heavy traffic. Chase, my mom, and my brother also drove in to spend the holidays with us.

Claire

I broke down when Marshall called and said traffic was too bad, and he couldn't make it for Thanksgiving dinner tomorrow. Heavy storms in Florida often make it difficult for people to travel. Roads become slick and lightning strikes are a big concern. Multiple car accidents have made travel near impossible for him. When I control my tears, I walk downstairs to join in the holiday festivities.

Daniel says, "Claire, we have our plane over at the airport. We could take you to Lake City to pick Marshall up, then bring him back here for the holidays."

I look at Daniel. "No, it's okay, but thank you."

"By plane, we could be there in less than an hour."

"Daniel, thank you. I don't want to put you out."

"It's no bother, really. Drew and I would be more than happy to do it. It looks like the storms have moved from the area."

I look around the room and everyone is here but Marshall. Even Skylar's mom and brother are here for Thanksgiving. I can see the sadness in my daughter's eyes and it hurts me to see her so sad. I don't want to put him out, but I also don't want to see Ava sad for one more second. It's the holidays, and families should all be together.

"Are you sure I won't be putting you out?"

"As long as we make it back before Thanksgiving dinner, it's no problem." Daniel smiles at me so I know it won't be a problem. Everyone laughs and it puts my concerns at ease. "Dinner isn't for another 18 hours or so, I'm pretty sure we'll be back by then."

"Get your coat, and I'll call Dad to let him know you're on your way so he'll be ready," Ava says excitedly.

"Skylar, do you want to come with us?" Drew asks.

"You're driving?"

"I'm flying if that's what you're asking, Dad will co-pilot this trip."

She grins. "You don't have to ask me twice, let me get my jacket."

We say our goodbyes to everyone and head to the plane. I'm impressed with the skills of Drew and Daniel flying the plane and I'm excited to be able to get Marshall and bring him back so he can spend Thanksgiving with his family.

"Well, it seems the problem with the traffic begins here," Drew says. Skylar and I look out the window. "Looks like traffic is backed up probably from a semi accident hauling hazmat materials." All I can see is a long line of headlights and taillights.

As soon as we land, I call an Uber driver to take us to the house. Drew and Daniel both stay at the airport with the plane, while Skylar rides with me to the house.

"I haven't heard from Ava. I sure hope she was able to get ahold of Marshall to tell him we're coming."

"I'm sure she did, and I'm sure he'll be excited to not have to spend Thanksgiving alone."

"You know, he was more worried about Ava being alone than anything."

We pull into the driveway and I can see the lights on in the house. Skylar says, "He didn't have to worry about Ava being alone."

"I know."

We arrange for the Uber driver to wait for us before we go into the house. When I open the door, Marshall is sitting on the sofa facing the front door, and a woman is sitting on the couch facing him. I stop at the doorway and Skylar bumps into me. The woman has a short brown bob haircut, and she's wearing jeans and Marshall's sweatshirt. I can't see her face, but I think I know who it is. Marshall stands when he sees me. Skylar walks around me so she can get a better view of what's going on.

"Oh," Skylar says.

Marshall looks worried. He doesn't walk towards me, but stands in place.

"What's going on?" I ask. I look at Marshall and then down at the woman sitting on our couch. She stands and turns around so I can see her.

"Oh, my God, Nichole."

She's holding a washcloth to her nearly swollen shut left eye. Her mouth is bleeding with a laceration across the top lip, and her face has dried blood on it.

"What happened?" I rush over to her and help her to a sitting position. "Skylar, would you get her a glass of water, please?" *I know I should wait for someone to answer me, but my mind is racing with questions. Has she been mugged? Why aren't the police here? Where's her car? How did Marshall get involved?* "What happened?" This time I sit down and wait for someone to answer me. Nichole is sitting beside me and I feel her trembling.

"I'm sorry, I didn't have anyplace else to go," she whispers.

I look at Marshall for answers and he can't give me any. He sits down on the other side of Nichole. "You don't need to be sorry, you're always welcome here." I look at her sadly.

She tries to smile, but is unsuccessful. "Thank you."

"What happened? Should we call the police or Brett for you?"

She shivers and I look at Marshall for answers. *Again, nothing.* Skylar comes into the room with a glass of water and another wet washcloth. "Put this on your lip. It'll help with the swelling."

"Thank you."

There's a car horn and I suddenly remember the Uber driver parked in the driveway. "I'll tell him to go on."

"Thank you, Skylar."

"No problem." She gets her wallet from her purse and leaves out the front door.

Suddenly, I remember Nichole's words. "I'm sorry, I didn't have anyplace else to go." I remember Ava's dreams of Connor abusing her. I remember Ava's X-rays of her broken wrist, broken ribs, and her front dental implants; all are consistent with her dreams of abuse by Connor.

"Brett did this?"

She nods her head and cries.

Ava

Skylar calls and tells me that they arrived safely, but they'll be late. She was very vague when she called. I have to wonder if air traffic is the problem. Is there even such a problem as air traffic on the holidays? Rachael, Xander, Chase, Skylar's mom, Jessica, Mark (Jessica's brother), and I cook, laugh, and have a great time. The house smells of cranberry and is filled with holiday cheer. The inn didn't have any guests for the holidays, so the families were each able to get a room of their own. When everyone turns in for the night, Xander and I watch a movie in his room. He looked tired this evening, but he refused to go to bed and rest. I didn't say anything to him, but he and Rachael exchanged looks that spoke loudly and clearly that she wanted him to go and rest.

I change my clothes and decide to wear something more comfortable. A pair of red plaid sleep pants and a white long-sleeved tee shirt is my outfit of choice. We lie on top of his covers and watch *Planes, Trains, and Automobiles*, starring John Candy and Steve Martin. We have popcorn and wine, and we laugh and cuddle. I like this movie, but some parts make me sad. Xander is very sensitive to my needs and is very sweet. Since I chose this movie, he insists he gets to pick the next holiday movie. He chooses something uplifting that he knows I will enjoy: a 30-minute TV special — *A Charlie Brown Thanksgiving*.

When the last movie is over, he takes his evening meds and I stand from the bed.

"Are you leaving?" he asks. I watch as he also stands from the bed. His adjusts his white tee shirt and plaid sleep pants. "I'd like for you to stay." Before I have time to say anything, he says, "Just for the night. I just want to hold you, nothing else."

I remove the pillows and fold back the quilt and the sheet on my side of the bed, indicating I'll stay. He smiles and mimics my movements. We climb in bed and I cuddle into him.

We talk about past holidays, family traditions, and this Thanksgiving holiday. We don't speak of the future, since

Xander's future is unclear. I'm assuming he'll be here for Christmas; I hope and pray he'll still be with us this Christmas.

The front door opens and we get out of bed to greet our families. "Looks like the slumber party ended before I was ready," Xander says.

I wrap my arm around his waist and stand on my tiptoes to kiss him. "There's always tomorrow."

"Story of my life," he teases.

We happily walk down the stairs, hand in hand, and greet the rest of the families standing in the foyer. "Hey, what took you guys so long?" I ask, stepping off of the last step. I notice there's an extra person with them, but I'm not sure who it is.

Rachael and Chase join us from the guest room. "We were beginning to worry about you," Rachael says sincerely.

The woman standing with Mom and Dad turns around. Her left eye is swollen shut with purplish coloring around it, and her lip, which is also swollen, has sutures in it. My heart drops to the pit of my stomach.

"I'm sorry, Ava. I didn't mean to ruin your holiday."

I look at the door, almost expecting to see Brett standing there, when I realize he may be responsible for this. "Oh, Nichole, don't be silly. You're not ruining anything. Are you all right?"

"I will be. I didn't want to come, but your mom and dad insisted."

I need to know who did this. "Is Brett with you?"

"No."

That's my answer. Brett is responsible for hurting her. "You're not ruining our holiday. You're always welcome, and I want you to stay for as long as you want."

"That's right, Nichole. We have room and you can stay here as long as you need to," Skylar confirms.

"Thank you. I just need a day or two to figure some things out."

"I'll make some tea," Rachael says. "Daniel and Drew, would you mind helping me?"

"I'll come with you," Xander says.

Once they are out of the room, I have to ask, "Did Brett do this to you?"

Her lip quivers and a tear falls down her blotchy face.

Dad says, "We took her to the hospital where they stitched up her lip, and she also filed a report with the police."

I shiver and close my eyes. Connor used to beat me, not that I remember, but there is proof of such beatings. Did he learn it from his dad? Is domestic violence inherited or learned or taught?

Opening my eyes, I ask, "Did they arrest him?"

Dad says, "Not yet. If they did, we haven't heard."

"You probably want to take a hot bubble bath," I say to Nichole.

"That would be nice, thank you."

"Room eight's empty." Skylar walks towards the stairs. "There's a clean robe in the closet, and there's some toiletries in the bathroom you can use."

"Thank you, I appreciate everything." She walks slowly behind Skylar to her room. Once she's out of view, Mom says, "I have an extra nightgown she can wear for tonight."

"She'll need something for tomorrow or however long she'll be here," I say. I hope she'll be here for a long time. I hope she won't cave in and go back to that jerk. I know people do. I think they love the person so much, they really want to believe them when they say "it'll never happen again." It usually does happen again, and the beatings are worse the next time. "She'll need something for the pain. I'll get her some hot tea and some Tylenol."

Nichole showers and I take her some tea and pain meds. She doesn't leave the room that night. Maybe it's from embarrassment, I don't know. She has nothing to be embarrassed about.

The next morning, Skylar's mom, Jessica, is already up. We run to Walmart to get Nichole some underclothes, a nightgown, and other clothing for a few days. When we get back, I start the coffee and put the turkey in the oven. As the coffee brews, everyone starts to gather in the kitchen, even Nichole. Her eye looks worse than it did yesterday. I don't say anything, and neither does anyone else. Mom and I set the coffee cups, creamer, and sugar out on the table for everyone. Skylar heats up the breakfast casserole in the second oven.

"I'm sorry I ruined your Thanksgiving," she says sadly.

I look at Nichole with a doleful look. "You didn't ruin our holiday."

"I didn't?"

"No, not at all. You're here, you're alive, the exterior injuries will heal, and you're making a step to better your future. I'm thankful for that. I'm also thankful that Xander and his family are here with us, and ..."

"We're happy that you're here with us this year, Ava," Mom interrupts.

Not everyone knows what she means by her statement, and I don't want to go into it. "See, we have lots to be thankful for today."

Nichole fills her coffee mug, "I guess we do. Thank you for having me."

"You're family, you're always welcome."

Chapter Two: Thanksgiving Joy or Holiday Terror

Xander

This Thanksgiving is different from the ones from my past. The past few days I've been feeling sorry for myself, but this morning Ava put things into perspective for me, for all of us.

Even with everything that Nichole and Ava have been through, Ava is still grateful to be alive and has found many reasons to be thankful. I know about Ava's memory loss, and I'm certain that this isn't the first time Nichole has been beaten by her husband.

This may be my last Thanksgiving, and I'm grateful to be spending it with Ava, my family, and everyone else in the house. Nichole's eye is swollen shut and is already black and blue from bruising. Her stitches to her top lip make it difficult for her to eat and drink, even with a straw, but she is still grateful to see another day. We all could learn something from her. There's a lot to be thankful for this year.

I thought that her husband would be calling her, begging her for forgiveness, but I haven't seen her on her cell phone once. Maybe he's already in jail and he won't be a problem for her. That's a nice thought.

As much as I would like to sit in the kitchen and watch Ava, I have work of my own I need to attend to. I have a book that I need to finish, and then I can rest and enjoy the time I have left with Ava and my family. I hope *Lost in Savannah* will be my best book ever. I like the title, but I have been thinking of changing it to *Dying in Savannah*. This book will have more meaning than any of my other books. This book I hope will say in writing everything I'm not yet able to vocalize in this life. I have so much that I want to say, but I can't find the words to tell Ava in person.

It's too soon to voice my strong, barely-in-control feelings. I know that. The way I feel about her would surely frighten her and she would run far and fast away from me.

I make my excuses to go to my room to rest. Drew knows my plan. I'm not sure he agrees with it, but he tolerates it. He feels I should be spending all of my free time with my family, and he's probably right. But my books are part of my legacy; after I die, they will live on. As soon as I get this book done, I will spend time with my family.

Before I can leave the room, Ava is right behind me.

"Are you okay?"

I look her in the eyes and her eyes hide nothing. Concern stares back at me. *I hate lying to her.* "I am. I just need to rest for a while."

"Do you want me to fix you some soup or tea and bring it up to you?"

I look at the countertop full of a Thanksgiving day feast that everyone is making and it makes me feel grateful for her. In the midst of all of this cooking and baking, she is willing to take the time to make me soup and tea.

"No, Ava. I'm fine. I won't be long."

"Rest as long as you need. If you're not up for dinner…"

"I'll be down in plenty of time for dinner. I just need an hour or so."

"Okay." She leans up and kisses me. "I'll see you in an hour."

I kiss her back and leave. When I go into my room, I leave the door partially opened because I want to be able to hear what's going on downstairs. Sitting in the chair I get on my computer and get right to work. The story and words are already in my head, I just need to transfer them to paper. Thankfully, the words flow easily from my mind to my fingertips.

There's a tap on the door and I close up my computer. "Come in."

"It's time you joined the festivities, don't you think?" Drew walks in and sits on the bed.

"Just finishing up."

"How's your book coming along?"

"I'm hoping to be done with it in a few days."

"You need a proofreader?"

My brother always proofreads my books. But this one is personal to me. "I think I'll send it off to Wesley and let him do the proofreading and editing this time."

"Okay, I get that. If you change your mind, let me know. Do you have the cover for it yet?"

"Not yet. I'm hoping to get the cover this weekend. I need something special, different, personal."

He stands from the bed. "I brought my camera if you want me to take some pictures for you."

"I was hoping you would offer your services."

"Just let me know when."

Nichole

When I'm not around people, I'm in my room attending to my injuries. Applying ice to my already swollen eye, taking Motrin for pain, and applying Neosporin to my sutures. I've had injuries like these before, and these aren't the worst I've had.

When I left my house after Brett hit me, I left with nothing, not even my cell phone. I knew he had a tracker on it, and I didn't want him to find me. He promised me he would never hit me again, and yet he did, again. I can't live this way. I don't want to, not anymore.

I had no idea where to go. It was the night before Thanksgiving. Marshall had seen my injuries before, so I went straight to his house. I knew he would help me without judging me. He wouldn't ask questions that I couldn't answer. Like, why didn't I leave sooner? My plan was to stay with Marshall and Claire for a day or two. I needed time to think about what I needed to do. What is the best way for me to leave? I know Brett and I know he won't let me go so easily. He'll beg and plead for me to stay. Or he might even threaten me. Either way, it wouldn't be good. I didn't expect Marshall to be home alone. Then Claire and Skylar showed up.

After I got the medical attention I needed, Daniel and Drew insisted there was enough room in their plane for all of us. I didn't want to come to Savannah, but I didn't want to stay in Lake City where I feared Brett would find me. At least here, I have a few days to think before Brett figures out where I am. Maybe by then I'll be long gone.

At dinner, we hold hands around the large dinner table while Daniel says grace. He thanks God for the food and for blessing us with life and second chances. It makes me miss Connor. I'm happy to see Ava is moving on, but the pain of losing my son will always be there. I'm still not sure what caused the fatal accident that claimed my son's life or caused Ava's amnesia. I never saw the police reports or the photos of the accident. Brett was in charge of all that and his funeral. He excluded me from everything. At the time I thought it was to protect me. Now, I'm not so sure.

Dinner is delicious and the conversation is pleasant. The conversation flows freely around the dinner table. There's no talk of politics, bombings, beatings, illnesses, cancer, or death. There's only talk of love, second chances, happiness, and new beginnings.

Ava looks happy and relaxed. I have to wonder if she could remember her past, would she be this happy. I feel terrible and guilty. Ava is sweet to be helping me. Sadly, I didn't help her when I should have. I think back on all of the times I wanted to help her, but couldn't. I couldn't help myself, so how could I help her? I guess seeing your father beat on your mother all through your childhood and adult life, maybe you think it's okay. I should have left the first time it happened. I thought I was doing my son a favor by staying. I didn't want Connor to be raised in a broken home. I also didn't want to struggle financially with a son. I wanted Connor to have the best life he could have, and I thought that would be in a home with a mom and a dad. That was my first mistake.

I eat slowly in order not to cause pain to my already sore mouth. Others finish eating before me, but no one moves from the table until the last person is done. I hear Christmas music that I didn't notice earlier playing softly in the background. I wonder if there's a reason for the holiday music playing and for the Christmas decorations being up earlier than usual. It's none of my business so I don't ask, I do comment on the great choice of music. I love Christmas music and in my opinion, one month isn't long enough to listen to it. I'd listen to it year round if I could.

After dinner and dessert we all gather around and watch an old classic movie: *A Christmas Carol.* It's the 1938 version starring Reginald Owen as Ebenezer Scrooge. I like this movie because a man changes his life and makes it better, much better. I have a chance to do the same thing.

The next morning when I wake up, the swelling is finally going down and my eye is beginning to open. I alternate between the Tylenol and Motrin for the pain and swelling. I shower, and dress in an outfit that Ava bought for me. The inn doesn't have any guests staying here; it's just family and friends. When I walk downstairs, I was expecting to see people in the kitchen, but it's empty. The coffee pot is half full and still hot. They must have just recently left.

Xander walks in and says, "Ava and Skylar went black Friday shopping." It brings a fond memory to my mind. "She wanted me to tell you there's coffee and a casserole on the stove if you're hungry."

"Did they just leave?"

"No, they left before the sun came up. Skylar said something about you being there before the stores open."

"Skylar's right. The stores carry only a few sale bargain items, and if it's something you want, you need to be there early." I smile as I remember the first year after I met Ava. Shopping on black Friday was a tradition of Ava and Skylar's.

"Not sure what they needed, but they looked like they were on a mission when they left this morning."

I fill a mug with hot coffee. "Do you need a warm-up?" I ask, looking at the mug he's holding.

"No, thank you. I've had all I can drink for one morning." He rinses his mug out before setting it in the sink. "I need to get some writing done. I'll be in my room working if you need me."

"Okay, I'll see you later."

Xander

While in my room writing, I hear arguing coming from downstairs. I stop typing and listen. I've been staying here for a few weeks, and I have never heard anyone even raise their voice in this house. When the voices escalate, I run downstairs.

Standing in the front doorway is Nichole. The front door is wide open. I stand back and observe before I make my presence known. I have no idea who is standing on the other side of the door, but I'm assuming it's her husband, the batterer.

When he grabs her by the arm, I step forward. "Get your hands off of her!" I yell.

He does and she steps back. "Are you okay?" I ask, stepping in front of her.

She nods, but I don't believe her.

"Come on, Nichole. I think you've been here long enough. I've come to take you home." He takes a small step forward.

I can see her shadow move further away from me. "Don't take another step into this house." I square my shoulders and puff my chest out.

"Nichole, I said, let's go!"

When she doesn't say anything or move, I turn slightly towards her. I don't want her to leave with him, but I can't make her stay against her will. The only thing I can do is hope she'll make the right decision. When I see the fear in her eyes, I have my answer.

"Go upstairs. I'll deal with him," I whisper.

She nods and walks quickly to her room on the second floor.

"Brett, Nichole's staying here. I've already called the police, and she's filed a restraining order against you. She also has an appointment with a divorce attorney on Monday." *These are all lies, but he doesn't need to know that.*

"You don't frighten me."

"And I'm not trying to. I'm letting you know the facts and this is how it is. You've hurt her for the last time."

"She needs me, she's nothing without me."

"Leave. She doesn't need or want anything from you."

He takes a step back. "We'll see about that. This isn't over."

Once he's gone, I walk upstairs where I find Nichole crying. *I hate seeing a woman cry.*

"He's gone."

She wipes away the tears. "He may have left, but he isn't gone. He'll be back." She cries again. "He's mad enough that the next time he'll hurt me."

"He already has, look at you."

"Xander, you don't understand. This is nothing. This," she motions to her face with her hands, "this is nothing compared to... what he's done." I never once considered that her beatings would ever have been worse than this. To imagine something worse than this sickens me. Now, I wish I hadn't been so nice to him. "I need to leave. He'll be back and when he does, he won't be the nice person you saw downstairs."

Nice? I thought he was a jerk. I don't want to imagine how bad this can get for her. Her face is full of fear. She came here with nothing. No money, no purse, and no clothing. *Where will she go?* I thought she would be safe here. I should have known he would find her.

"As soon as Ava and Skylar get back, I'll move you someplace safe. He'll never find you." Before she can say anything, the front door opens and I hear giggling. "When you're ready, come downstairs. I have a plan."

"Thank you for being here with me today, Xander. I don't know what would have happened if I had been here alone."

"Let's not think about that. Dry your eyes and meet us in the kitchen when you're ready."

I help Ava and Skylar carry all of their purchases into their living quarters. They laugh and are in a great mood. Drew, Marshall, and Dad come in from cutting down an old tree from the back lot, Mom, Claire, and Jessica are reheating leftovers in the kitchen, Mark is outside on his cell phone playing Pokémon Go, and Chase walks in with his laptop from an outdoor seating area.

The atmosphere in the house is light and happy. I don't say anything about Nichole. When Nichole gets down here, I won't be able to hide the fact that she's upset or the reason for it. She takes longer than I thought to come downstairs. Her eye is still badly swollen and very bruised. It's even painful to look at. I can't imagine what she went through in her marriage. She said the next time he'll hurt her. I'll never understand why a man would or could hit a woman. I know it happens, she's living proof. When she finally walks into the room, she looks visibly shaken and upset. Her eyes are red and puffy, and her pale face is blotchy.

Ava notices first and rushes over to her. "Are you okay?"

"Brett was here," Nichole stutters.

"What? How could he have found you?" Ava asks.

Marshall steps forward, "Did he hurt you?"

She shakes her head. "Xander was here and stopped him."

All eyes are on me. "He came to take her home."

"That asshole can't be serious!" Ava yells. It's very seldom that Ava uses curse words; I like her feisty spirit. "He's out of his freaking mind. There's no way in hell you're leaving and going back with him."

"Ava," Nichole whispers, "he'll be back and he'll cause problems for everyone in the house."

"Let him! The prick doesn't scare me." *I have to wonder if Ava has always been this brave.*

"Or me," Skylar says, but not as convincingly as Ava.

"He'll cause problems for your guests," Nichole says.

Ava and Skylar remain quiet. Now they understand this could be a potential problem for their business. "I have an idea," I say. I look at Mom, Dad, and Drew. "I think Nichole should use my house since I'm staying here." I know my family was hoping I would be returning home soon. I feel fine and I want to spend some time here at the inn with Ava. "When I return home, I can stay at the beach house on the property." *If I make it home and my cancer doesn't kill me first.*

"Xander, I couldn't...."

"Nichole, I think that's a great idea. Xander's house is just sitting empty. There's no telling how long he'll be here with Ava," Dad says. "It'll give you some time to get your affairs in order. Then when Xander returns, you can move into the beach house if you need more time."

I can see when Nichole realizes she doesn't have any money. Chase says, "Just give me a go ahead and we can freeze his bank accounts and start your divorce proceedings."

For the first time since I met her, I can see hope on her face. "You can do that? Freeze *his* bank accounts?"

"As long as your name's on them, they're joint accounts. A judge will also give you some money from those accounts to help get you settled." He smiles slightly. "I just need the go ahead to get things started. If we can hurt him in his wallet, he may be persuaded to leave you alone."

Her lips quivers and she nods. "Thank you, Chase."

"Let me get to work on this. A couple of photographs will also help your case. Would you mind?"

"I'd rather not, but if it'll help."

"Trust me. It will."

I watch as they both leave the room. Ava hugs me and thanks me for helping Nichole by letting her stay in my house. How could I not help her? I'd buy her a house if it means she won't be returning home to that scumbag. "So this means you'll be staying here with me for awhile?"

I plan to stay here with you for as long as I can. "A little while longer," I say instead.

Ava

Chase worked all weekend and did exactly what he said he was going to do. He got Nichole some money and froze Brett's bank accounts. He also got her a restraining order and started with her divorce proceedings. Everyone thought it would be best to get her out of the area, so Drew, Daniel, and Rachael flew her to their home in the Outer Banks. Daniel and Rachael thought it was best that Nichole stayed in their beach house instead of Xander's house. I guess Daniel knew that Brett was a dangerous man.

On Monday everyone who was here for Thanksgiving is gone and it's back to business as usual. I'm glad and excited that Xander is staying longer than he originally planned. He seems to be doing well, although he naps daily. When Drew left, he and Skylar made plans to see each other this weekend. I'm excited for her and I'm happy to see that she is seeing someone I approve of. Drew is like Xander in many ways, and not just looks. You can tell their mother *and* their father had a big influence in their upbringing.

During Xander's naptime, I walk the second floor and check each of the rooms. I thought he would be asleep, but he's up and working on his computer when I walk past his room. "I thought you were napping?" *He looks guilty.*

"No, I couldn't sleep. Thought I might as well get some work done."

"You're writing a book?" I ask, walking further into his room.

He closes his laptop. "I am."

"You don't nap when say you're going to, do you?" He has very honest eyes. He scoots over and I sit on his bed beside him.

He smiles. "I can't say I do."

"You spend your time writing?"

"I have a deadline." I cringe at the irony of his words. "Sorry. I want to get this book published as soon as I can."

I know that Xander wasn't given long to live, but he seems to be doing so well. Maybe it's false hope, but sometimes I think the doctors are wrong. I want to say, "You have plenty of time," but I say, "Are you almost finished with it?"

"I was hoping I would have been done over the weekend." I nod. I know the weekend isn't what any of us expected. "Hopefully tomorrow."

"Good, I can't wait to read it."

"Do you want to go down to River Walk with me one night this week? They're having their Christmas lighting festival."

I smile. "It's a lot of walking for you. How about we do one of the tour trollies, instead?"

He looks concerned. "Are you worried about me?"

"I am. I don't want to tire you out with all of that walking."

He thinks before saying, "Okay, I'll come up with something that doesn't require much walking, but it won't be a tour trolley kind of date."

"You have something against trollies?"

"No, not at all. I just want something a little more special for our date. Something more memorable, perhaps."

"It's a date." I laugh.

"What's so funny?"

"It's like we live together, but when I say it's a date, I realize we really aren't living together at all."

He thinks for a moment. "We're very comfortable together, aren't we?"

"We are. I wouldn't have it any other way."

"Good, me either. Now git, so I can finish my writing."

I stand from the bed. "Okay, will I see you for dinner?"

"Are we having turkey?"

"God, I hope not."

"Good, then I'll be there."

"I'll make us a homemade pizza."

"Sounds good, and maybe we can watch a movie later."

When I leave Xander's room, I make sure I leave the door cracked slightly. If something happens, I want to know. He has a doctor's appointment coming up next week and I pray for good news. I know his cancer is terminal, but when he seems so healthy, it's hard to grasp the idea that he's dying. *Dying? Is this even possible? I want more time with him. I want to see where this relationship is going.* While Xander writes his book, I decide to google his type of cancer. I want to fix him. I don't want him to leave me so soon after meeting him. It isn't fair. Life isn't fair.

I'm sad when there isn't any hope, or a slim chance of hope. The risky surgery is his only chance, and it's a very slim chance. *Any hope is better than none, isn't it? His mother said he was more afraid of the risks of the surgery, than of dying from the cancer. I get that, I think. Maybe. But if there was a chance you could live, wouldn't you want to take that chance? Remove the tumor and live the rest of your days able to do what you want. I know he's afraid of being left in a vegetative state after the surgery. I know it's selfish of me, but I want him to take that chance. I would be right there by his side either way, wouldn't I?*

Skylar worked the tearoom today while I researched Xander's cancer, then she left to do some Christmas shopping. Finally, I close my computer and start making the pizza dough from scratch.

Xander walks into the kitchen wearing his signature smile. He saunters over and brushes some flour off of my cheek. He bends down and kisses me sweetly. "This is a good look for you," he whispers.

I instantly get goosebumps. "Thank you. Did you finish your book?"

"I did."

"Really?"

He steps back and laughs. "Why are you so surprised?"

"Because it takes years to write a book, doesn't it?"

"For some people. I already had the main idea in my head, I just had to put it to paper. I'm one of those authors who don't suffer from writer's block."

"May I read it?" I ask excitedly. *We're in a relationship. It's okay that I ask to read his book early, right?* I smile and collect the pizza dough from the bowl.

"When I get it back from my editor, you can."

"I can?"

"Yes, I would like to know what your thoughts are."

I am beyond excited and I try hard not to show it. "Do the main characters get a happily ever after?"

He looks serious. "No, do they need one?"

My heart drops. *Yes, they need one. He's a romance writer, he should know this. You can't have romance if there's not a happily ever after, can you?* I toss the dough in the air and catch it. "I just hope you don't disappoint your biggest fan." *I hope he hasn't seen the movie* Misery *or read the book. In it a writer kills off his main character, thus making a happily ever after impossible. His biggest fan holds him hostage and makes him rewrite the book.*

He smiles. "Maybe I need to do a re-write."

Maybe you do. "It's your book, do as you see fit." Xander puts on an apron and flours his hands before scooping up the extra dough in the bowl. He watches me before he tosses his dough in the air. I watch as it goes higher than it should and falls through his fingertips as he attempts to catch it. He cringes and I laugh.

"I don't think you're supposed to puncture the dough."

"Maybe I should stay out of the kitchen and stick to writing."

I place my dough on the pizza pan. "Here, add the toppings while I try to fix this mess," I tease, picking up the dough from the bowl.

"Now this is something I can do. Before I forget, make sure you're available Wednesday night. For date night."

I smile. "Okay, it won't be a problem."

After we eat, we sit down and watch a movie. His first mistake is to let me pick the movie. *You've Got Mail* is my all-time favorite movie, and I've never missed an opportunity to watch it. As you would expect, it has a happily ever after. I think it's like a boxer listening to the theme of *Rocky* during his workout. It's a given, right? His second mistake was to let me cuddle into him during the movie while on a full belly.

Xander

As soon as I wrote the last word in my book, I sent it off to my friend and editor, Wesley. I thought about letting Ava read it, but quickly decided against it. This book is personal to me. It's my story and when she finally reads it, she'll truly know who I am and what's in my heart. I hope my true feelings don't frighten her.

Ava sleeps through most of the movie and I let her. I'm disappointed when she wakes up. I was hoping she would sleep until morning so I had an excuse to hold her all night. I haven't known her long, but I have this longing or desire when I'm near her. Who am I kidding? I have a need and a desire to be with her when I'm not near her. She's special and now that my book is done, I want to spend every second I can with her.

She adjusts her eyes to the television as the credits roll up the screen. I watch as she blinks when she realizes she's slept through most of the movie. She yawns before sitting up. "I'm sorry. I didn't mean to fall asleep. Did you enjoy the movie?"

"It's one of my favorites," I lie.

She giggles. "You're a terrible liar."

"I was too busy watching the beautiful girl sleeping on my shoulder. I didn't really notice anything else."

She jumps as if she's frightened or scared. "Your meds! You forgot to take your meds."

I reach on the end table and rattle a bottle of pills. "Took them."

She holds her hand over her heart. "Thank you, God."

"Don't worry. With God's help, I have everything under control." *Well, not everything. But my meds, I definitely have those under control.*

"I know you do. I just worry."

Of course she does. "I should leave since you have house guests. They'll be expecting a gourmet breakfast at sunrise."

"I hope not." She stands from the couch and I stand with her. "They'll be disappointed on both accounts. Nothing gourmet gets served from this kitchen, and I'm barely awake at sunrise." I look at the clock and realize I have nothing to do. Normally, I would work on my book, but since it's done, I have nothing to do.

"What's wrong?" she asks.

"I think it's the first time in my life that I don't have anything to do."

"It's bedtime. You don't need anything to do."

I laugh. "I'm not tired."

She looks at me and she gets a big smile on her face. "I'm not tired either. Do you know how to play chess?"

Say it isn't so. A girl who likes chess. It's almost too good to be true. "I do."

"But are you any good?" she asks.

I cough. "I've won a game or two." *Should I tell her I was in a chess tournament in high school? Nah, I'll keep that to myself.*

"Come on. Show me what you got."

"I'd love to."

I follow her into her bedroom and watch as she pulls a box down from the top shelf. "We should play in here, since the game could last several days. Do you have a problem playing in my bedroom?" She bats her eyes and I laugh.

I swallow to keep from choking on her choice of words. I watch her to see if her words could have a double meaning. "Are you going to use it as a distraction?" *Please say yes.*

She laughs and rolls her eyes. "You wish."

Yes, I do. She removes a stack of books from a round table in the corner of her room before setting up the game.

"Do you need help setting up the pieces?" I ask.

"Why? You don't think I know where these little things go?" She wiggles a black pawn in her hand.

I laugh. "Just trying to be a gentleman. That's all."

"No, I have it." She bends over to place the pawns in a row, and I try hard to not look. Now, I'm positive she's going to use her... assets as a distraction.

Finally I walk over to the other corner of the room to get a second chair for me to sit on. "When you're done playing with those little pieces, let me know. I don't have all night."

She laughs. "Okay, smart ass. Game on."

Ava is far better at chess than I ever thought she would be. She's quite competitive and fun to play with. At 2:00 am I decide it's time for us to call it a night. Her competitive side wants to keep playing, but her rational side knows she needs to get to bed. She has a business to run. "I feel bad for keeping you up so late."

"You should," she teases.

"Because I feel responsible, I'll help you with breakfast."

"Good, I'll see you at 6:00."

Wait? What? "6:00?"

"That's right. We start early to make sure everything's ready."

I look at the clock, and it's already after 2:00. "Okay, I'll see you in a few hours." I turn to leave with no intentions of being here at 6:00 am to help cook breakfast.

"Not so fast." I stop and turn around to face Ava. She throws a blanket and pillow at me and says, "Sleep on the couch so I can make sure you're up."

I catch the flying bundle of bedding. "What? I'm crushed that you actually believe I would stand you up."

"Save it." She rolls her eyes again. I laugh as I walk out of her bedroom. "You weren't coming back in the morning, were you?"

"Wasn't planning on it," I say, shutting the door behind me.

I sleep on the couch as she instructed, or should I say, I try to sleep on the couch. It's hard to sleep knowing that Ava is just a few steps away. I replay the relaxed fun evening we had and the constant smile on her face is imprinted on my mind. When I hear screaming coming from her bedroom, I stand just as Skylar runs through her bedroom door. She startles when she sees me in their living quarters but her focus is on Ava. "She's having another nightmare," she says as she runs past me in her nightgown.

Another nightmare? I didn't know Ava suffered from nightmares. I'm right behind Skylar and Ava is sitting up in bed with tears streaming down her face.

"Was it about him?" Skylar asks.

Him? Who's him?

Ava nods.

"Was it the same dream?"

Ava wipes away her tears. "No, it was a new one."

"Let me get you some water."

Skylar leaves and I sit on the edge of Ava's bed. "What was your dream about?" I ask as softly as I can.

She cries as she clutches the pillow on her lap. When she doesn't answer me, I ask, "Can I hold you?"

She removes the pillow and leans into my arms. I can feel her body tremble. Whatever the dream or nightmare was, I know it was pretty bad. "It's okay, you're safe now."

"Here's your water, Ava. Are you all right now?" Skylar asks as she walks closer to the bed.

"I will be. Thank you."

"Okay, I'm heading back to bed. Xander, stay with her."

Skylar leaves, Ava lies under the covers, and I lie on top of them and hold her closely. "Are you ready to talk to me about your dream?"

"Do you know how I know Nichole?"

I think about past conversations and I can't recall ever hearing how they all know each other. *I take a wild guess.* "Friends of the family?"

"No. Nichole and Brett had a son named Connor. Connor was my husband."

"She was your mother-in-law."

"Do you remember I told you about my amnesia?"

How can I forget. "Yes, of course."

She closes her eyes and says, "I have nightmares that my husband used to hit me." I don't move. "He once pushed me down a flight of stairs."

"You dreamed this?"

She nods her head and opens her eyes. She looks sad. "I have a scar in the same place where I was wounded in my dream, so I went to my doctor and he did x-rays and a CAT scan of my body." *Please don't be true.* "Do you see these front teeth?" she asks.

I smile to lighten the mood. "I do and they're beautiful."

"They're not mine. They're implants."

I instantly feel anger. "He knocked your front teeth out?"

"He also broke some of my ribs and my right wrist, and I have a few scars on my scalp."

"Oh, Ava. I'm sorry. I had no idea."

"Sometimes I have nightmares about some of the fights Connor and I had."

"Are they memories?"

"Some are. I'm not sure about the others."

"The nightmares are usually the same ones, but tonight... it was different."

"Another fight?"

"It was the night of the accident." She shivers, so I hold her closer. "We argued about someone's kid or kids, he hit me, and then we wrecked."

Like father, like son, I think to myself. *If this is true, that bastard deserved to die.* "I'm sorry, Ava. I'm here and I'll protect you." I kiss her on her forehead and hold her close. "I'll always be here to protect you." *Well, I'll be here for as long as God lets me.*

Ava

When I wake up, the sun is shining brightly. I get out of bed in a panic. Xander isn't beside me. *It's late. I slept in. I never sleep in.* I hear laughter coming from the dining room. Our guests are up. I rush into Skylar's bedroom and she isn't there. *Good. Maybe she's in the dining room with the guests.* I want to go out there and see what's going on, but I can't face our guests looking like this. She and Xander must have gotten up and made breakfast. When I walk into our kitchen, the coffee pot is on. I try to calm the panic of sleeping in. I know Skylar has things under control, and possibly Xander, too.

I pour my coffee and sit at the breakfast bar. Only a few guests were here for the night. Maybe it wasn't such a task to prepare breakfast for so few people. Still, Skylar shouldn't have had to do it by herself. I'm upset with myself for not being up to help them.

When I hear the outside door open, I'm shocked when I see Xander walk into the living quarters. I thought he was out there helping Skylar. I could have sworn I heard him talking.

"Good morning," he greets me warmly.

"Hey."

He walks over and kisses me.

"My alarm didn't go off this morning."

He sits down beside me. "I shut it off. I thought you needed your rest."

I'm a little upset. If he wasn't going to help Skylar prepare breakfast, he should have woken me up to do it. "I would have rather been up to help Skylar. I hate that she's out there on her own." I stand up so I can shower and at least help Skylar with the cleanup.

"I was going to help her, but Drew was here."

"Drew? What's he doing here?"

"I have no idea. It's none of my business." He laughs.

It's none of my business either. "I need to shower. I'll be out in a few minutes."

"I'll wait if that's okay with you?"

"Sure, it's fine."

I text Skylar before showering. I knew she and Drew were interested in each other, but wow, I had no idea they were becoming an item. He spent the night with her; I assume that means they're an item. I'm also assuming they slept together, so there must be something between them. Xander stayed with me last night and we weren't intimate. Maybe I'm jumping to conclusions.

Ava: *Is Drew here?*

I shower, dry off, braid my hair, and dress in warm clothing. It's a brisk November morning. I check my cell phone for a text from Skylar.

Skylar: *He is. Come out and join us. The guests are all gone for the day.*

She doesn't say why he's here. She's an adult. She doesn't have to answer to me, or tell me anything about her personal life, does she? Why do I even care if she has an overnight guest? Because Drew and Xander are brothers, and I was seeing Xander first. I don't want something to happen to cause conflict between all of us. If she dates Drew and it ends, will it be awkward between all of us? We've never dated brothers before, and now that we live together, I fear this might be a problem. B

When I finally walk out of the bathroom, Xander, Drew, and Skylar are sitting in the living room in our living quarters. Everyone's laughing and looks genuinely happy. *Ava, you worry for nothing. Relax and enjoy the time you have left with Xander.* The thought of losing Xander to cancer causes an instant crushing pain in my chest. If Xander dies and Skylar continues to date Drew, will I be reminded of Xander every time I see him? I force a smile when Xander looks up at me.

"Hi," I say to everyone. Xander pats his lap for me to sit on, and I do.

"Drew and Skylar are going to watch the inn this evening for our date," Xander says as he runs his hand up and down my arm. "I asked them to come with us, but Skylar reminded me someone needed to be here."

"If you guys wanted to come with us, we could always ask Lou Ann and Steve to house sit for a few hours this evening," I suggest.

Skylar says, "We thought about that, but we'll probably be better off just alternating date nights."

Alternating date nights? How long is Drew going to be here? Since Skylar and I are both single, this may work out for the best.

"I knew being inn keepers could be a problem for when we started dating. Alternating date nights could be a quick fix to this problem."

"Maybe on occasion we could hire one of the cleaning ladies or Lou Ann and Steve could watch the inn for nights we double date," Xander suggests.

"That's a great idea," Skylar says excitedly.

I have to agree. The bell over the main door rings, alerting us someone is coming into the inn. "I'll get it." I stand and walk out of the living quarters and into the bed and breakfast area. A woman is standing there with two small children.

"Hi, I'm Ava. May I help you?"

"Ava Emerson?" the woman asks.

I look at her to see if maybe I can recognize her. I don't. "Yes."

"Hi, Ava." She reaches her hand out for mine. "I'm Olivia. These are my twin daughters, Abigail and Emily."

I shake her hand before acknowledging her identical twin daughters. I kneel down to look at each child to see if I can tell them apart. Although some twins are identical, there's always a distinguishing factor to tell them apart.

I say to them, "Hi, I'm Ava." They look embarrassed and look away from me. I stand and gently stroke their soft brown hair. "How can I help you?" I ask Olivia.

"You don't know us, but I wanted to personally thank you for the gift cards and the check you sent us a while back." I look at her and I have no idea what she's talking about. I have to wonder if Mom and Dad didn't do something and put my name on it. When the confusion is apparent on my face, she says, "We've been staying in a shelter for battered women. I was going to send you a thank you letter, but I wanted to meet the person with such a kind heart in person."

I remember the article in the paper of the woman being dragged from her house nearly naked by her live-in boyfriend as he beat her. A man stopped his car, called the police, and rescued the woman and her two children from the drunken abuser. The paper didn't mention names or ages of the woman or the children. I sent the kids a gift card from Toys-R-Us and sent the woman a check. Not a significant amount; I just wanted to do something nice for them, and to the man who rescued them. My face and heart soften as I remember the article. Sometimes I wonder what would happen if I were to be put on trial for being a Christian. Would there be enough evidence to convict me? This gift card and check are some evidence that I would be proud to have used against me.

"How are you?"

"Better. Everyday gets better and everyday gets easier." She smiles.

I look outside and I don't see a car in the driveway. "Did you drive here?"

"No, I don't have a car. We took a bus and walked here from the closest bus route."

The nearest bus stop must be a half-mile away. I look at the table and it's cleared off, but the food is still out on the buffet. "Are you hungry? We still have food from breakfast and I haven't eaten yet."

"No, we couldn't, but thank you."

I watch Olivia, and I can see she thinks she'll be putting me out. The two girls we hired to clean come in and get some breakfast before they start their morning routine. I look into the chafing dishes and there is plenty of food. *Of course there is. Skylar and Drew set out way too much food for the few guests we had this morning.*

"It'll go to waste unless someone eats it." *It's not a lie.* "Please? I'd love to chat with you some more." It's already after 10:00 and it's almost too late for breakfast and it's too early for lunch.

Skylar comes out and says, "Ava, are you going to eat or should I clean this up?" She looks from me, to the woman, then to the two small children. "Oh, I'm sorry. I didn't know you were busy."

"Skylar, this is my friend Olivia, and her twin daughters, Abigail and Emily."

"Hi, it's nice to meet you," Skylar says, smiling.

"Thank you, and it's nice to meet you."

I hear two voices that sound identical coming from behind Skylar. Drew and Xander come in.

"I'd hate to waste all of this food. I might have to eat again," Drew says. *I'm not sure if he's teasing or if he's serious.*

"Olivia, this is my boyfriend, Xander, and..." I look at Skylar and smile. *If she's sleeping with Drew, they must be boyfriend and girlfriend, right? Then that's how I'll introduce them.* "And this is Skylar's boyfriend and Xander's twin brother, Drew."

I didn't get the expression I was hoping for from Skylar *or* from Drew. Maybe they are a couple. I watch as Olivia realizes there are two sets of identical twins in the same room. I look at the girls and their baby dolls they are holding, and they are also identical.

"Twin brothers?" she asks.

"Yeah, but I'm the good-looking one," Drew teases.

We all laugh. "Olivia has identical twin daughters, Abigail and Emily."

Skylar says, "I always wanted twin daughters."

Wait? What? She did? I didn't know that. Maybe I did and I just can't remember it.

"It's a handful," Olivia says. "But I love them to pieces."

"You should join us for breakfast," Xander says. "Ava and I haven't eaten yet." *I thought he ate earlier this morning. Was he waiting to eat with me?* When she looks uncertain, he says, "It'll just go to waste. Really, you'll be doing us a favor."

Olivia smiles and says, "Are you sure?"

I step closer and say, "We're positive."

Everyone gets a plate of food and drinks, before gathering together around the table. Olivia's twin daughters eat but they seem shy. I wish I had some toys for them to play with. They hold their baby dolls closely with one hand while they eat with the other. The girls are dressed identically with the same white bow in their brown hair.

"How old are your daughters?" I ask.

"They'll be four in another month."

"Christmas babies?" Drew asks.

"No, Abi was born on New Year's Eve, and Emi was born a few minutes later on New Year's Day."

I don't think I've ever heard of this ever happening before, although I'm sure it has. "Wait? So your identical twins don't share the same birthday or the same year, and they're a year apart?"

"Crazy, right?" Olivia laughs. "They're actually three minutes apart, but it was enough time that they were born in separate years, making Abi a year older than her identical twin sister, Emi."

"They'll have a lot of fun with that when they're older."

"They will." Olivia smiles. "But I'm afraid when they get older, it'll be a two-day-long party. In a few years, Abi will probably tell Emi, 'When I was your age, I…' and then say what she was doing a few minutes earlier."

Skylar looks at Drew and asks, "When's your birthday?"

I look at Xander because I have no idea when his birthday is. "It's May 17th," Drew says. I'm shocked when it's the same day as Skylar's. Skylar loves her birthday, and she thinks it's awesome when she knows anyone who shares her special day with her.

"Mine, too," she squeals.

"When's yours?" Xander asks me.

"February 27th."

Xander picks up his phone and adds it to his calendar. "Now I'll never forget it."

No one asks how Olivia and I know each other. It's obvious that I don't know her very well from the questions we ask back and forth.

They stand to leave and I walk them out to the front porch. "Thank you for everything and for the breakfast. You're very kind and we appreciate it."

"You're welcome. I'm glad you stopped by. You have a lovely family."

"Thank you. It's just my girls and me."

I'm relieved that she isn't with the boyfriend whom I read about in the paper. "You said earlier that you're still staying at the shelter?"

"We are. John, he's my ex, he's still living at the house we shared. I'm actually moving back to Texas next week. I like the area, but there's nothing here for my girls and me."

"You have family in Texas?"

"My mom and dad are there. I need to get going, but thank you for everything. It was very kind of you and I'll never forget it."

"You're very welcome, Olivia. Do you need a ride home?"

"No, the walk will do us good. Besides, it feels good to be out and about."

"Okay. Thank you for stopping by with the girls. It was nice meeting you."

The girls and Olivia turn to leave and I watch them until they're out of view. I'm so glad she's picking up the pieces and moving on without her abuser. She is definitely making the right decision.

Xander

When Drew and Skylar leave, Ava tells me the story about Olivia and her children as we clean up the breakfast dishes. Of course I knew that domestic violence existed but I guess I wasn't aware how prevalent it is. Why do men feel the need to beat on women and children? If I so much as thought about raising my voice to a woman, I have no doubt I'd be answering to my dad. No matter what age I am, he'd step in and talk some sense into me. Thinking back on my childhood, I don't think I've ever heard my dad raise his voice to my mother. Sure, they'd have disagreements, but it never escalated to anything more than that. I remember once when they were arguing, Dad got a Coke out of the refrigerator, poured it into two glasses, and gave my mom one of the glasses. I knew early on that my home life was loving and desirable. We had many friends, and our house was the gathering place for everything and anything.

Once the dishes are done, she makes a list of things she needs to get from the local store. When the afternoon tea is set up, and Skylar and Drew aren't back, I tell her she can leave and I'll be more than happy to run the tea.

"You think you can do this?" she asks, unbelieving. "Are you feeling up to it?"

"I feel wonderful." I look at the small buffet with the food, the flavored tea bags, and the teapots and dishes. "Refill the food and hot water as needed, clear off the dirty dishes, and collect the tips. Yeah, I think I can do this."

"Don't count on that many tips." She laughs.

I was just joking about the tip part. "Go, I can handle this. Drew and Skylar should be home any minute now."

She looks around before nodding. "Okay, call me if you need me."

"I will. Do I need to wear an apron or a name tag or something?"

"No, only if you want to."

Bending down, I kiss her. "Now go before I change my mind."

"I'll be back soon."

"Just be careful."

While she's gone, I clear the tables, refill the food and water, and chat with the women having tea. They don't need anything; however, they are very chatty. I don't recall Ava talking this much to her guests. When Skylar and Drew return, she immediately takes over the tea.

I look at Drew and remember that he went home yesterday. "So, should I assume you're seeing Skylar?"

"You should assume that I like her."

"Will this be a problem for us?"

"For me and her us, or you and me us?"

He's such an ass. "You and me us."

"No, it'll be fine. I really like her."

"Good. I really like Ava and I don't want you messing it up for me."

"I won't."

"Oh, good God, Grace. There's two of them." Drew and I both turn in the direction of the woman's voice. Standing there are two of the women who were having tea.

We both stand and greet the women. "Did you enjoy your tea?" I ask.

"We did. Now which one are you?"

"I'm Xander. I was waiting on you in the tearoom. And this," I turn to face Drew, "is my brother, Drew."

"Identical twins?" the other woman asks.

"Yes, Ma'am. We are."

"You see that, Grace? Twins."

"Mable, I got eyes, don't I? Xander, when do you work next?" Grace asks.

"I was just helping out my girlfriend," I say.

"He's here everyday," Drew adds.

Thanks, Drew. "Will we be seeing you tomorrow?" I ask.

"No, we can't make it tomorrow, but maybe Friday. Will you both be here on Friday?" Mable asks.

I speak up before Drew does. "Drew will be here for sure. I may be out with my girlfriend, Ava."

Grace says, "I've heard that identical twins are very close, beginning with or even before birth. Is that true?"

"Mom says that when we were infants, we wouldn't sleep unless we were next to and touching each other."

"Well, Drew, I hope to see you on Friday," Grace says.

Drew smiles. "I hope to see you both, too."

"Be careful going home," I say.

"Thank you, we will."

When they leave, Drew and I walk inside. I text Ava to make sure she's okay.

Xander: *About done?*

Ava: *Leaving now.*

Xander: *See ya soon.*

We both help Skylar clean up from the afternoon tea. When Ava pulls up and honks her horn, we all go outside to greet her. She has several items in the trunk of her car that she needs help to carry into the house.

When everything is in the house, I ask, "Does anyone care if I go take a nap?" I can see the worry in everyone's face. "I'm just a little tired, that's all."

"You can sleep in my room if you want," Ava offers.

I look at her and then look around the room at Skylar and Drew. They are now focused on the snacks that Ava bought. I doubt I'll get much rest in the living quarters, but I jump at the chance to be near Ava. "Sure, thanks."

"Yeah?" she asks with a big smile.

"I'd like that."

"Good. I'll try real hard to be quiet."

"You're fine, I just need to rest for a few minutes."

When I lie on her bed, I inhale her scent on the pillowcase. It smells of cranberry and vanilla. It reminds me of my childhood. In fact, it reminds me of every wonderful memory from my childhood.

I didn't think I'd be able to sleep, but when I wake up it's getting dark outside. Disoriented, I adjust my eyes to my surroundings. *Ava.* The clock reads just after 5:00 pm. It's not as late as I had originally thought. The time change still messes with me. I'll never understand daylight savings time or the reason for it. It seems to get dark earlier and earlier. When I leave her room, everyone is in the kitchen cooking. Skylar and Drew are making something together with fruit, while Ava is stirring a pot of something over the hot stove.

The gifts from earlier are gone and the living quarters looks just as it did before Ava came home. "Did you sleep well?" Ava asks.

"I did. Is there something I can help with?"

"No, we have everything under control."

"I need to take my meds, I'll be right back." I stop and turn on my heels. "Are we still on for our date tonight?"

"I went ahead and made dinner while you slept. I wasn't sure what time you'd wake up. If you still want to go out, I'm sure Drew and Skylar will take care of this."

Although I appreciate her effort, I'm disappointed I won't get the chance to take her out this evening. "There'll be another time." *I hope.*

When I go upstairs to take my meds, I call and cancel the reservations for this evening. I had dinner reservations at Carla Jo Dean's restaurant and I also reserved us a horse and carriage to pick us up at the restaurant and take us around River Walk, the city market, and several of the park squares. Although I'm disappointed about the date, I'm not disappointed about having dinner with Ava at the house. Anytime I get to spend with Ava, I know it'll be a great time. I don't know how much time I have left with Ava, so I need to make every minute count.

We have spaghetti, salad, and some kind of apple dessert that Skylar and Drew made. It's nice sitting with Ava, my brother, and Skylar around the small four-top round table. The conversation flows easily. When my vision gets blurry, I blink it away. It could just be a side effect from the meds. I'll just remain seated until it passes. When no one seems to notice, I'm thankful. I know my time here is limited, and it's going by far too fast. *I want more time with Ava. I need more time with Ava. I wish I had found her sooner, so I would have had more time with her.*

I talk to my oncology doctor often via e-mail and on the phone, but I think it's time I see him in person. My symptoms are changing, and not for the better. If my vision clears up tonight, I'll email him requesting an appointment; if not, I'll call him in the morning. I have an upcoming appointment, but I don't think it's soon enough.

Ava and I haven't had time to talk much today about her nightmare last night. I was hoping to find out more about her marriage and her husband. The more I think about it, the more I think her amnesia could be a blessing to hide such horrific memories. *Can a person live through such violent acts? Of course they can, but can they actually move on and live a happy life knowing what they've been through? I hope so. For Ava's sake and for Olivia's sake.*

Drew says, "I was thinking about taking Skylar on a horse and buggy ride through the park squares this weekend." I look at him with a glare. Of course he would. That was my date I had planned for Ava. He had no way of knowing that's what I had planned. I guess great minds and identical twins think alike.

Ava says, "I always wanted to go on one of those. I think it'd be so romantic." I hold her hand beneath the table.

"Babe, that sounds like so much fun." Skylar leans in and kisses him.

"Yeah, Drew, I think it'd be a great time, especially this time of year."

My vision cleared up and we all help with the dinner cleanup. Drew and Skylar are a lot more intimate than Ava and me. I wonder if their relationship isn't just physical. That's okay if it is, they're both adults. But it's not what I want with Ava. I want something with more meaning. *Why? I won't even be around this time next year.*

"I should let you get to bed. Thank you for dinner and I'll see you first thing in the morning."

"Xander?"

"Yeah?" When she doesn't say anything, I say, "What is it, Ava?"

"Would you mind staying with me tonight?"

Would I mind staying with her tonight? Is she crazy? I wanted to stay with her since the first day I walked into the inn. My next thought is why? She isn't the type of girl to just invite a man into her bed. Then I remember her nightmares. "I'd love to." And no truer words have ever been spoken.

I shower before bed, making sure I have everything I need with me. It's a small area, and I don't need to be walking around in a towel looking for something on my first night staying with Ava. Ava wanted me to stay with her, but I'm pretty sure it wasn't for a romp in the sack, aka Disneyland for adults. But I wouldn't judge her if it was. Is this going to be awkward? Should I offer to sleep on the couch? Should I plan to sleep on top of the blankets? I want to make love to her, but is it too soon? *Not according to Drew and Skylar, it's not.*

When I come out of the bathroom, Ava is already in bed reading. She's wearing a white tank top, and has the bed sheet and blanket pulled back on my side of the bed. Good, she wants me in her bed. I usually sleep in my boxer briefs, but tonight, I'll sleep in my sleep pants. She sets her book down and watches me walk across the room.

"What?"

"I've never seen you dressed in pajama bottoms before."

"Maybe because I hardly ever wear them."

She doesn't look away, but continues to watch me.

I smile internally. *She's looking at more than my bottoms.* I get into bed and cover myself up to my waist.

She cuddles into me.

Lowering my lips to her, I softly kiss the crown of her head.

She looks up at me with her black hair and dark eyes. She looks stunning. I bend down to kiss her and it's soft and sweet. Then it turns deeper and more intimate. She moans and it's sexual. She runs her hands through my hair and I kiss her harder. She moans and says, "I want you, Xander." Slowly, I roll over her and look down at her. "Are you sure?" I ask. Normally, I wouldn't ask, but I want to make sure this is what Ava wants. God knows, it's what I want.

"Yes, please. I want you," she whispers.

Chapter Three: Love and Health

Xander

Last night was one of the best nights of my entire life. If I die today… I'll still be pissed that I didn't have more time with Ava. I don't understand one-night stands. Why wouldn't you go back for seconds, or thirds or some number in the thousands or tens of thousands? Once I think about it, I'll never have enough time, or times, with Ava, no matter how long I live. She's a caring and giving lover. I wanted everything she had to give, plus some. But if I die today, I'll be thankful I had this one moment with her.

I felt like I couldn't do enough for her. I wanted the night to last an eternity. I wanted all of her orgasms, I swallowed every sexual cry through our intimate kisses. I wanted to be the last person to make her feel that way. I wanted, and want, to make her mine for the rest of our lives.

Ava was meant to be mine. She fit me like a glove and I loved every second of it. When we were done, we showered together and made love again. Is it possible to fall in love with her after just one night? It was more than sex. It was more than anything I've ever experienced. *Is it because I'm dying? Is this how women feel after sleeping with a guy for the first time? B*ecause of my death sentence, I realize how precious life is, and I know how short a lifetime can be.

I lie awake, holding Ava closely to my bare chest. Her breathing is shallow and soft. She smells of sex, vanilla, and cranberries. Even while cuddled together, she fits into me perfectly. I don't think that I sleep at all this night. I just lie awake and replay the night over and over in my head. I don't want to forget one sound, one movement, one word that came from her sweet lips. I want to remember it for the rest of my life.

The rest of my life reminds me of how little time I have with Ava. A few months, less than a year. It's already been almost two months. I'm not ready to go, I want more time. I need to fight harder, try harder, and be healthier. I need to see my doctor and talk to him about other options, maybe get a second opinion. Is it wishful thinking that he's wrong? That he's made a mistake in my diagnosis?

I need to get home to see my oncologist. I need to see about other treatments, other surgeries, and other medications that are available to me. I'm not ready to give up just yet. I'm strong and feel well enough, so maybe I can fight this. Maybe I'll be one of the few who can survive terminal cancer. If not, maybe I can extend my life a few more years. I need more than a few measly months to be with Ava.

When Ava's breathing changes, I'm afraid she's beginning to dream. I'd be damned if I'll let the bastard enter her life again, even if it is through a dream. "Shhh, baby. I'm here with you," I whisper into her ear. "I've got you."

She cuddles deeper into me, and I let her. I vow to keep her demons at bay for as long as I can. If I run into that bastard in the afterlife, I swear, I'll kill him all over again. Hopefully, we won't be in the same place.

Ava

Xander is everything I imagined he would be. Kind, gentle, and passionate. I'm so glad that we finally made love. I know we've been out on only a few dates, but I've spent so much time with him over the last couple months. He's always here and we share almost every meal. I see him daily and we've become close.

People may judge me and think I made a quick decision, but they'd be wrong. Seeing him every day for months has let me get to know him quite well. After the night we just spent together, I want to get to know him more. I want to know everything I can about him. I want to see his baby pictures, read his yearbook comments from his classmates, know about his past relationships. I want to know about his likes and his dislikes, his favorite foods, and what he wants out of his life. It may be short, but I want to know what I can do to make the rest of his life better.

I want more time. I need more time with him. I know surgery was his only option and he quickly declined it for fear of what could happen. But… what if it went well, and it cured him? What if tonight was the first night of many years that we will spend together? I need to talk to him. I need to convince him that the risk is worth it. I need to show him that I'm worth the fight to get better. That I'm worth the risk of the surgery. That living for today isn't the answer. That he needs to seek a future.

I cuddle into him and sleep better than I have in months. This is definitely my safe place.

Xander

When I know Ava is in a peaceful sleep, I get out of bed and text Mom. I tell her I need to come home and I ask her if she'll call Drew in the morning and tell him that she needs to see us. He'll worry if I tell him I need to return home. He might also bitch about having to leave Skylar. But if Mom says she needs us to come home, he'll leave at a moment's notice to be with her and to help with whatever she needs. I just need to get home to see my oncologist about my vision and about alternative treatments. I have this newfound need to live.

Ava and I shower together and just before breakfast, Drew's phone beeps that he has a text message. I already know it's Mom, but I pretend to be clueless. Ava and I fill the coffee carafes while Skylar removes the casserole from the oven.

"Mom needs us, we gotta go."

I look up with what I hope is a surprised look on my face. "What's wrong?" I ask.

"She probably needs a bookshelf moved," he teases.

Skylar and Ava observe, but remain quiet. "She didn't say what was wrong?" I try to sound concerned.

"All she said is that she needed to talk to us."

"Well, we better get going if we want to make it back by this evening."

"Xander, don't forget your meds." I look at Ava and I'm not surprised that she would be concerned for me.

"I won't, Baby. I'll be home tonight if I can. I hope her *talk* won't take too long."

"You stay as long as she needs you. Family first," she says, sincerely.

She's got that right. Family is always first. Drew and I help the girls and make sure the food and drinks are set up on the buffet before we leave for our trip home. I don't want to be gone from Ava, but this is something I need to do. I kiss and hug her before leaving. She looks sad. *Does she think this is a one-night stand? Shit. This is terrible timing for me to have a revelation about living.*

"I'm sorry, this is terrible timing."

She smiles slightly. "The timing is a little off."

"I'll do my best to be back tonight, but if not, hopefully tomorrow. I still owe you a date." I stroke her full, soft lips with my thumb.

She smiles and I hope she knows that I'm serious. "Try for tonight."

"Okay, I'll call you later today to let you know what's going on." I look over and see that Skylar and Drew are having their own intimate conversation.

"All right, but I'll miss you." She leans in and kisses me. It's a kiss different from the other kisses we've shared before last night.

We fly out to the Outer Banks and when we get to the house, Mom has some lame jobs for us to do. Just as Drew said, she says she wants her bookshelves moved from one room to the other. Just as we start to remove the books from the shelves, Mom and Dad call me out of the room. Drew doesn't say anything, he continues to work.

When I walk into Dad's study, I close the door behind us. He sits behind his desk and interlocks his fingers beneath his chin. "Your oncologist called, he can see you today."

"Good. I was hoping he would."

"Your mother tells me you're having problems with your vision."

"I am."

"She'll go to your appointment with you, and I'll help Drew with the bookshelves." He looks at Mom. "Maybe we could just move them to another wall in the same room? I don't want to spend the entire day moving bookshelves."

I interrupt. "There's something else."

"Oh, Xander." Mom sounds heartbroken. I know she worries about me. I know that after what happened to Drew a few years ago, she can't stand the thought of going through that again.

"I want to talk to the doctor about the surgery, or another progressive treatment." I can see hope on Dad's face and tears in Mom's eyes. "I'm ready to fight. I wanna beat this."

Mom places her hand over her heart. "Oh, Xander. What changed?" Mom asked.

"Ava's what changed his mind," Dad says.

"Did she talk you into the surgery?"

"No, Mom, she didn't. She doesn't know that I'm here to talk about my treatments or my conditions."

"Then what changed?"

"I like her. I've been thinking about it and I want to go at it as aggressively as I can."

"Have you fallen in love with her?" Dad asks.

There's a knock at the door before the door opens. "Come on, Xander. I need help moving the bookshelves."

Dad stands and says, "Xander's going to help your mom, so it looks like you and I are moving the bookshelves today."

"Are you feeling all right?" Drew asks.

I hate to lie to him, but I don't want to worry him, either. "I'm fine. Going to the store with Mom."

He watches me as if he can read my mind. *Thank God, he can't.* "Okay, I'll see you in a bit."

When Drew and Dad leave, Mom says, "Come on, we better get going to make your appointment."

Ava

I had the most amazing night with Xander last night. He brought emotions out of me that I didn't know I had. He was everything I was hoping for and more. When he said he had to leave this morning, I was sad. If I could imagine what a one-night stand felt like, I'm afraid that this would be it. I tried hard to not focus on that feeling. I know it was just poor timing. Certainly, Xander felt the same way I did, didn't he?

We have breakfast and we always have lunch here at the inn. Today, Skylar and I bake Christmas cookies and scones for the tea. I think since Drew and Xander are gone, we're just trying to stay busy. "Do you think they'll be back this evening?" Skylar asks.

I hope so. "I'm not sure. Xander said tonight or tomorrow. I guess it depends on what their mother wanted with them."

"It's weird not having them here, isn't it?"

"Yeah, I guess it is. You really like him, don't you?"

Skylar looks dreamy eyed, and this is not a look I see on her very often. "I do. We have a lot in common, and he's great in bed."

I look at her and we both bust out laughing. "I didn't need to know that."

"You're my best friend and I had to tell someone."

Still laughing, I say, "I swear, if you go into detail, I'm leaving." Just then the phone rings and I'm excited to see it's Xander. Skylar's phone also rings, and when I see her smile I know it must be Drew. We walk to opposite ends of the living quarters before answering.

"Hey," I answer.

"Hey, yourself. How is everything?"

"Skylar and I spent the morning baking."

"Sounds like a good day."

"It is. How's your day?"

"Good, running errands with Mom. She sends her love."

"Aww, tell her I said 'hi.'"

"I will. I just wanted to hear your voice. I'll call later when we get back to the house."

"Okay, sounds good. I'm glad you called."

"I miss you."

"Me, too. I'll see you soon."

When I'm done on the phone, I set the food for our lunch out on the counter. Skylar is still in her bedroom on the phone. I'm halfway through lunch before Skylar joins me. She's happy and smiling. It's great to see her happy, and in a relationship. *Is she in a relationship? It's moving so fast between her and Drew. You can sleep with someone and not be in a relationship with them. It must be a relationship, right? Whatever it is, she's happy, and that makes me happy.*

After lunch, I say, "I'll work the tea if you want to leave to do some shopping or something."

"Ava, you wouldn't mind?"

"No, not at all. Christmas is coming and we need to get out and shop when we can."

"I do need to get some things. Are you sure you don't mind? I always feel like I'm bailing out on you."

"Don't be silly, and don't feel like that."

"Okay, if you're sure. Can I ask what are you getting Xander for Christmas?"

Am I getting Xander anything for Christmas? "I don't know. I haven't given it much thought."

"Well, you better hurry. You'll run out of time soon."

"I guess you're right. I don't know him well enough to know what he would like or want," I admit honestly.

"Well, you could always ask him." She leaves the room and returns with her jacket, keys, and her purse. "I'll see you later, if you think of something you need while I'm out, call me."

"Okay, I will. Be careful."

"Always."

Later that night, we don't get a call from Xander or from Drew. I'm worried but I don't say anything. If Skylar's worried, she doesn't say anything either. We sit in the living quarters while I read, and Skylar flips through the television channels. "Screw this, I'm calling Drew." Skylar stands up with her cell phone and walks into her bedroom. When I hear a car pull up, I stand up and walk out into the main foyer. I'm hoping it's Xander and Drew, but I'm expecting it to be a guest checking into the inn.

When I don't recognize the car, I open the door to greet our guests warmly. Getting out of the car are two men: Xander and Drew.

"Hey, sorry, we don't have any vacancies," I tease.

"It's okay, my girlfriend's the co-owner. She said she could squeeze us in." Drew smiles as he slings a duffle bag over his shoulder.

The screen door opens and Skylar hops off the front porch and runs into the waiting arms of Drew. I envy her easy-going spirit and her relationship with Xander's brother. I've been seeing Xander longer and I'm still not that comfortable with him yet.

I walk off the porch and go to Xander. He smiles, never taking his eyes off mine. "It was rude of us not to call, but…"

"It's okay, I'm just glad you're here. Everything go well with Rachael?"

"It did." When I get closer, he steps forward and wraps his arms around my waist and leans down to kiss me. "I tried to get here sooner."

"I've missed you," I say between kisses.

We start to walk in the house, and I soon realize that this isn't the car they left in this morning. "Whose car's this?"

"It's mine," Drew says.

"Where's your truck?" I ask Xander.

"It's still at the airport."

"You drove home from the Outer Banks today?" Skylar asks.

The guys look at each other. "It's a long story, but Dad's flying in tomorrow."

I look at Xander for him to elaborate. "I'll explain later."

That answer is good enough for me. Drew unpacks his duffle bag quickly before we watch a movie and have popcorn before going to bed. The movie is *Edge of Tomorrow*, an excellent Tom Cruise action/adventure film that did well but could have done better at the box movie if the subtitle — *Live Die Repeat* — had been its main title. Tom keeps fighting aliens and dying, and then coming back to life while retaining his previous memories. He progresses from an incompetent newbie who dies in a couple of minutes to an incredibly competent warrior who is hard to kill. And the kickass romantic interest is played by Emily Blunt.

In the middle of the movie, Drew asks, "Does anyone care if I remove my prosthetic leg? It's been itching me all evening."

Wait? What? Prosthetic leg? I honestly had no idea. Without faltering, Skylar says, "No, babe, go ahead."

I look around and Xander and Drew are looking at me. "No, I don't care." I sound surprised although I try hard to sound casual.

Drew doesn't move to remove it. "You didn't know about my injury?"

If someone had mentioned it, I would have remembered. "No. It's never been mentioned."

Drew looks at Xander, who says, "It's not my story to tell."

I respect Xander for not talking about his brother's personal life. "What happened? A car accident?" I ask.

"Kind of. My Humvee got hit by two improvised explosive devices in Iraq."

He's military? That's another surprise. "Oh, my God, Drew. I'm sorry. I had no idea. I'm truly sorry."

"It's all right. Everyone else in the vehicle died; I was the sole survivor."

Skylar shuts the television off and holds Drew's hand. Xander also holds my hand.

"I was the lucky one."

I wanna cry for Drew and the soldiers who lost their lives fighting for this wonderful country we live in. In this world, soldiers don't come back to life, unlike the movie we're watching. I wish I had a heads-up on this news about Drew. I want to say something worth hearing. I had no idea that Drew had a missing limb. He walks perfectly fine. There was nothing to make me think that something was ever wrong.

"I'm sorry you had to go through such a traumatic event, Drew. I'm sure it wasn't easy losing your… friends."

"That's right, Ava. They were so much more than my comrades, they were my dear friends. Losing my leg was a very small price to pay." Skylar rubs Drew's arm. "I went into the military with a 20-year plan; I was going to retire and then fly an aircraft professionally."

"Things change, huh, brother?" Xander asks.

"Yeah, they sure do. Not always for the better either."

Xander becomes sad. "Could've been worse. It could've been your funeral I attended after the Humvee explosion."

Xander

We don't finish the movie, and Drew doesn't remove his prosthetic leg either. We talk about Drew's short military career, and how he suffered from depression, PTSD, and survivor's guilt.

Ava opens up about her amnesia, her deceased husband, and about her haunting nightmares that have proven to be memories. Drew is very sympathetic and says, "Sadly, I don't think amnesia would be such a bad thing in my case, or even in your case."

"I know. I often remind myself of that. I wish I remembered the good things about my life. The years prior to meeting Connor; the years I had with Skylar and Chase."

"I get that," Drew says. "That would totally suck to forget the good things in your life. I wouldn't for anything in this world want to give up my memories of the guys who lost their lives."

We say our goodnights and just before bed, I talk Ava into taking a bath with me. I have something I need to talk to her about, and I'm not sure how or when to say it. Maybe a bubble bath, and some wine, will help.

Once we are in the tub full of bubbles and I begin to relax, I say, "I have some pretty important news to tell you." I can see fear in her eyes. I don't like seeing her frightened, so I decide to just tell her. "I've decided to fight the cancer." When she doesn't say anything, I continue. "I met with my oncologist today, and he wants to fight the cancer aggressively with stronger chemo and radiation before operating."

"Oh, Xander." She scoots closer to me, straddles my lap before kissing me. Water slops over the edge of the tub, but I don't care. When the kisses stop, she asks, "What changed your mind?"

"I've recently realized that I have a lot to live for."

She smiles slightly. "You're talking about me?"

"I am."

She feathers kisses all over my face. "This makes me extremely happy." *The side effects of the aggressive chemo and radiation and the complications of the surgery are still a concern for me.*

"When will this begin?"

"Dad's flying in to get me tomorrow."

"That soon?"

"I want to do this while I'm still healthy enough to fight it."

"They need to shrink the tumor before they can operate on it," she says, not really talking to me but more like thinking out loud. "You'll be staying at home and going to the hospital everyday for your treatments?" she asks. She watches me and I can almost see the wheels churning inside of her head.

"I'm not sure if I'll be home or staying at the hospital. I didn't ask that. I do know I'll be pretty sick from the aggressive treatments. Then when I finally have the brain surgery, I'll have an intense recovery time… assuming it goes as planned."

She looks sad. "Don't talk like that." Before I can say anything, she says, "I want to go home with you and help you through this. I want to be with you." *I wasn't expecting that. Having Ava come and stay with me when I'm at my weakest, I'm not so sure I like this idea.* "Drew's staying here with Skylar, isn't he?"

"I think so."

"I saw him bring in a duffle bag today." She looks at me with hopeful eyes. "Maybe he wouldn't mind helping her here with the inn, while I go and stay with you?"

"Ava, I'll be pretty sick. You might want to think this over."

"I have thought this over." She thinks for a minute without looking at me. "If he says no, I'll ask Mom to come up and stay. She'll be more than happy to help out."

She has it all worked out. "Okay, let's dry off and we'll ask Drew. If he declines your lovely offer about being a co-innkeeper, we'll call and ask your mom." Ava's already getting out of the tub and drying off before I finish my sentence.

I get out, dry off, and follow her out of the bedroom wearing a pair of basketball shorts. Ava's wearing a short cotton robe. She taps on Skylar's bedroom door. "Can we come in?" she asks, opening the unlocked door. She's braver than I am. Knowing my brother, he's lying butt naked on top of the covers. I stay and wait for an invite before walking in.

"What's up?" Skylar asks.

I walk into the bedroom to find Skylar and Drew already in bed. They both have books sitting on their laps and each of their bedside lights are on. Ava looks at Drew's prosthetic leg propped up against the wall before she looks at him. "Are you going home tomorrow with Xander and your dad?"

"Xander's leaving tomorrow?" Skylar asks.

"I've decided to go forward with the surgery."

Her eyes light up with approval. "Good for you. I think you've made the right decision."

I look at Ava. "Yeah, me, too."

Drew sits up straighter in bed and says, "No, I wasn't planning on it." Skylar looks over at Drew but she remains quiet. He says, "I'll be there for the surgery, but I don't see any need to be there for the treatments leading up to it."

"I would like to be there for that." Everyone looks at Ava. "I know it's a lot to ask, but would you mind helping Skylar run the inn during my absence? If it too much, I can ask Mom…"

Drew interrupts. "No, Ava. That's not necessary. You don't need to call and ask your mom to help out. I was planning on staying here with Skylar for as long as she'll have me. It only makes sense that I help out when needed." *Where is Drew and what has Skylar done with him?* "As long as she doesn't mind showing me what I need to know."

Ava turns around and smiles at me before turning around to face Drew. "Thank you. I promise I'll take good care of your brother."

Drew laughs. "And I can't make any promises that I won't burn down your kitchen."

The next day, things move along more quickly than I expected. Dad came to get us at noon, and the doctor arranged for my aggressive treatment to start as soon as possible. Ava quickly changed from my girlfriend to Nurse Emerson. It's nice knowing she's taking such an interest in my care and treatment. I wanted to show her around the house and the city where I was born and raised, but she's more interested in seeing where the hospital is, where my pharmacy is located, and what street my doctor's office is on. She adds all of the important phone numbers into her cell phone.

Since dating will soon prove to be non-existent, I insist on taking Ava out to dinner at a restaurant called Port O' Call in Kill Devil Hills. It's one of my favorite places to eat and I think Ava will like it. I know that once I start the chemo and radiation, I won't be up to doing much of anything. I also know that these next few days might be the last good days I have with her. I know I'll die without the surgery, and I may die with it. I also know I'll become very sick with the treatment and this quite possibly might be the last real date I'll ever have with her.

We have an intimate dinner for two in a private room I reserved earlier in the day. The room is normally hard to get, but it helps to know the owners of the restaurant. After dinner, I also arranged for a horse and carriage ride so we can look at Christmas lights in the downtown area. We're served hot chocolate with marshmallows and given fleece throws at the start of the ride. The downtown is beautifully lit with colored and white Christmas lights. Christmas music plays and it reminds me of my childhood. Once that is done, we take a walk on the beach behind my parents' house. I asked Dad earlier if he would stack a pile of firewood for me on the beach with some matches, kindling, and a couple of blankets. I didn't want to leave Ava and take the chance that she would come looking for me. I wasn't ready to reveal my plans with her just yet. Dad does everything I ask plus he provided a small basket with champagne, cheese, crackers, and fresh fruit. We make love in the sand, stay warm by the fire, talk until morning, and then watch the sunrise. She smells of cranberry and vanilla and I never want to forget her unique scent, or this night.

When the last of the firewood burns out, we walk up the steps past the small beach house. Nichole's inside having coffee. She smiles and waves as we walk past and up to the main house. Mom is making breakfast, while Dad sits at the breakfast bar reading the newspaper.

"Good morning," I say.

Ava looks embarrassed as if Mom and Dad know what we did on the beach last night and earlier this morning.

"Breakfast will be ready in about thirty minutes if you two want to freshen up," Mom says with her back to us. Dad is still reading the paper, not paying any attention to anything going on in the room.

"Okay, we'll be down in a few minutes."

As soon as we're upstairs, Ava whispers, "I think she knows we just had sex."

I want to laugh. Mom had her back to us, why would Ava think she knows something? "She does not. And if she did, I'm pretty sure she doesn't care." I laugh, but Ava doesn't find any humor in any of it. I'm a grown man who just stayed the night on the beach with a beautiful woman. Now that I think of it, I'm sure Mom knows something was going on. Dad, too.

"It's embarrassing."

I take her by the hand and lead her into my bedroom. "Come on, let's shower. I'm starving."

She quickly releases my hold on her. Still whispering she says, "I can't shower with you. Where's the guest bathroom? I'll shower in there."

Grinning, I say, "Have it your way. Meet me downstairs when you're done."

"I'll hurry," she says.

We both get done about the same time. Ava wears and needs very little makeup and her hair is braided in a wet braid down her back. She's wearing a hoodie and a pair of black yoga pants when she walks into my bedroom.

"Are you ready?" she asks.

"I am." I turn off the light and Ava holds my hand as we walk down the large staircase. I hold onto the railing and hold her hand with my free hand. We have breakfast and Nichole joins us. It's good seeing her and she looks better than the last time I saw her. She tells us that Chase is doing an excellent job as her attorney and that so far, Brett hasn't been in touch with her.

"What will you do once your divorce is final?" Ava asks. "Your possibilities are endless."

"It's funny you should ask that." Nichole wraps her hands around her hot coffee mug. "I was actually thinking of moving to Savannah. I always wanted to open a bakery and I found a building for sale that has an upstairs apartment. The downstairs was used as a bakery until they recently closed."

I say, "Why they closed would be my concern." Although I don't want to add unsolicited advice, I feel this needs to be addressed.

"I googled it and it said there was a death in the family and the owners moved back home to Wisconsin or someplace."

"Wasn't from a lack a business. That's good." *If the bakery failed from lack of business, another bakery in the same location would more than likely also fail. No sense in repeating their mistake.*

"Skylar and I love the area. I think having a local bakery there would be a great investment. Will you be making scones, macaroons, and no-bake oatmeal cookies?"

Nichole smiles. "For you, Ava, I'll make whatever you want."

"Good. I'll need lots and lots of no-bakes."

I put it to memory that Ava likes no-bake oatmeal cookies. They are one of the healthier cookies. The conversation flows easily, and Mom and Dad seem to like Nichole and enjoy her company. I personally think it'll be a good idea to have her living closely to Ava. If something happens to me, I want to know that Ava has family or friends nearby. Even if Nichole is Ava's ex-mother-in-law. I want to know that Ava will be taken care of and surrounded by people who love her. It makes me sad thinking that I may not be around much longer, but it gives me all the more reason to fight like hell to beat this battle with cancer.

Ava

When Xander's oncologists said they wanted to treat his tumor aggressively, they weren't kidding. The chemo and the radiation are making him nauseated and fatigued. During the first few days, he would eat and sit up with his family to watch a movie, but now, after five days, he doesn't get out of bed. His external radiation is done; however, he is still taking the internal radiation and strong amounts of chemo.

I stay in bed with him and sometimes we talk, but most of the time he sleeps. When he sleeps, I eat, then I return to his bed with him. I wanted him to fight this, and I'll be right here with him. I'm trying to be strong for him, but the day I removed a clump of his beautiful dark, curly hair from his pillow, I cried.

I thought this is what I wanted. I never dreamed it could be this bad. Just last week we made love on the beach, but now, he can barely get out of bed. I have never seen someone deteriorate so quickly. I thought I read and researched everything there was on his tumor, the treatment, and the prognosis. *Did I miss something? Did I not research something?*

His mom and dad sit in his room with him everyday. They talk to him about his childhood and about his family. They tell him how much they love him and how proud they are of him. I listen and stay cuddled into Xander. I listen to his heartbeat and memorize his breathing pattern. His mother updates Xander about his book sales and personal e-mails from his readers, and she relays messages from his friend and business manager, Wesley. I'm not sure Xander can hear her, but she continues to talk to him as if he can. I remember Mom telling me that she would read to me when I was in a coma. I can remember that I wanted to talk back to her, but I couldn't. When I woke up from my coma, I was so grateful she never gave up hope that I would come back to her.

Drew comes home today and stays in the room with Xander. He tells me that Mom is there helping Skylar. I suspect that Rachael called him to come home. Xander's lost most of his hair, he's weak, and he looks thin and sickly. He looks nothing like the strong, handsome man who walked into my bed and breakfast just a few months ago. Drew cries and it pulls my heartstrings. He tells Xander to fight, to not give up. He tells Xander he's nothing without him. I cry, Rachael cries, Daniel and Drew also cry. Seeing Xander like this is almost too much to bear.

In the middle of the night, I wake up to Xander twirling my hair with his finger. I cuddle into him and let him hold me.

"Hi," he rasps.

"I've been worried about you," I say honestly.

"I know. I can hear you cry."

I tilt my head and look back at him. "I'm sorry. I'm trying to be strong."

"I know, I can tell."

"I suck at it. I'll try harder from now on."

He leans in and kisses my forehead. "Can you help me to the restroom and maybe get me something to eat?" he asks.

"You're feeling better?"

"I will as soon as I use the restroom. I'm so thirsty."

I help him to the restroom and offer to make him anything he wants to eat. When he wants only jello, I'm not surprised. I wake up his mom, dad, and Drew so they can visit with him since he's awake and feeling better. Xander goes in the hospital tomorrow for testing to see if his tumor's shrunk. I'm hoping this is a good sign that it has.

Xander visits briefly with his family before he becomes sleepy again. When they leave and I get back in bed, he tells me he needs to see Nichole in the morning. I find it odd, but I don't question it. If he wants to see her, I'll make sure he does.

The next morning, Daniel and Drew help Xander shower. Nichole is here for breakfast and she's looking better than she did the last time I saw her. I'm glad for her. Everyday she's healing physically and I hope emotionally.

"Xander wants to see you," I say, taking a sip of my hot coffee.

"He wants to see me?" she asks.

"That's what he said."

"I'll stick around until I see him. I can't imagine what he'd want to talk to me about."

"I have no idea." I prepare her so she won't be surprised by Xander's appearance. It's more for his benefit than it is for hers. I don't want her to be shocked when she sees him. I don't want her to look at him any differently. This is hard enough on him. Even I'm surprised by his rapid deterioration.

I offer to help Rachael with breakfast, but she quickly declines my offer. It's taking Xander longer than normal to shower, and I wish I had something to keep my mind off of waiting for him. When Xander, Drew, and Daniel walk into the eat-in kitchen, they are all different — they suddenly have become bald because they have shaved their heads. Daniel is holding Xander by his arm to support him. Xander still looks sickly, but he's smiling. He stops near the barstools and looks around the room.

I fight back the tears at the show of support they are showing for their son and brother. I stand and smile.

"Triplets," I tease, walking right to Xander. He may look exactly like his brother, and he may also resemble his father, but there is no confusing the three.

"This is a look I haven't seen in awhile," Rachael says happily. Well, as happily as she can make herself sound.

I have to admit that the haircut looks better than the straggling pieces of hair he had earlier. I kiss Xander and help him to sit in the nearest chair to him. Sitting beside him I ask, "You've seen this look before, Rachael?"

Rachael walks over, wiping her hand off on her apron. "It was when Drew went into the military. They all shaved their heads to show their support for Drew and the Army."

I instantly remember Drew's prosthetic leg and it saddens me. This family has been through so much, yet they still manage to wake up with a smile most of the time.

"It's a good thing the Jamison men can sport such a unique look," Nichole says from a distance.

Xander turns to look in her direction as if it's the first time seeing her. I wonder how he didn't see her when he walked into the room. Normally, he would stand to greet a woman in the room, but today, he's just too weak.

"Good morning, Nichole," he says.

"Good morning, Xander."

Xander leans in and whispers, "I need to talk to her in private."

In private? I knew he wanted to see her, but I had no idea it was going to be personal. "Can you talk here while I get your breakfast, or do you need a room with more privacy?"

"No, here's good. I just need a few minutes." I lean in and kiss his dry lips. "Okay, I'll stall at the stove for a while."

"Thank you, Ava."

"It's okay. I'll go and get her for you."

I walk back and see the sadness on Nichole's face. "Xander's ready to talk to you." I walk away from her and walk over to where Drew, Daniel, and Rachael are standing at the stove. Rachael is filling everyone's plates when Daniel turns to fill the five juice glasses. I turn to look at Xander talking to Nichole. I know that the treatments that Xander is taking are making him tired and weak, and I sure hope it'll all be worth it. Maybe he was right thinking that the quality of life is more important than the length of life.

When Nichole looks over at me, I look away. Xander wanted to talk to her in private, and the least I can do is give it to them.

"What time is his doctor's appointment?" I ask.

"His appointment's at 11:00 am."

My stomach flips at the possible news we'll get today. That Xander might need to go through another week of aggressive treatments is painful to think about.

After breakfast, Nichole leaves and we all get ready to go to Xander's appointment. I spend more time than necessary getting ready. I need time to prepare myself for the news. I need to play out each possible outcome in my head and figure out the next step. I need to be strong for Xander and for his family. Before we leave, I text Chase and tell him I'm thinking about him. I haven't seen him much over the last several weeks or has it been months? However long it's been, it's been too long. I miss him. I miss his positive outlook on life, his easy-going, laid-back personality, and his smile. Before we leave, he texts me back.

Chase: *I miss you, too. Seems like Thanksgiving was eons ago. I'll make time to see you before Christmas. How's Xander?*

Ava: *We'll know something soon. Leaving now for his doctor's appointment.*

Chase: *Okay. Hope it goes well. Chat later.*

Ava: *Okay, I'll try to call you later.*

We wait patiently in the treatment room while they do Xander's CT Scan and X-rays. No one says anything, but I can't help but notice the occasional sniffles from his mother. They rip right through my heart. I stand and look around the blank canvas of a room. No soft colors on the walls. No calming ocean sounds coming from the tape player. No soft glow from a lamp and no scenic portrait on the wall to look at to take your mind off of the possibly grim news we may get. Just cold, stark, and industrial views to remind us of why we are here. A tear falls and I quickly swipe it away. I don't want to show my sadness. I just met Xander a few months ago, and I need to be strong for him and his family.

Xander returns from his testing, and now we have to wait to see the doctor. Seconds tick by as they turn into hours, possibly days. I look at the clock and it's been only 37 minutes. *Can that be right?* Xander sleeps and it reminds me that time is against us. How much time do we have? I know he can become too sick to have the surgery. He was healthy just a week ago. This fatigue is from a side effect of the medications, right? When Xander becomes nauseated, his brother rushes to find a nurse and an emesis basin. I stay close and offer comfort. *Internally, I'm screaming at the doctor to get here and give us some answers. Haven't we waited enough! At least give Xander some answers so he can go home and rest.*

When Xander throws up in the emesis basin, his dad stands angrily and leaves the room. Rachael wets some paper towels and dabs them on Xander's face and neck, while I hold another emesis basin to Xander's mouth. Drew stands by with a wastebasket. The only thing I can think about is cancer sucks, and how much I hate this for Xander.

Chase

I was glad when Ava texted me today. I just saw her on Thanksgiving, but I didn't get to spend much time with her. She had a house full of family members and then we had the issue with Nichole and her husband Brett. Nichole took first priority over everything else.

The more time I spend with Ava, the more I wish I could tell her how I feel. I watched her with Connor, and now I'm sitting and watching her relationship bloom with Xander. "The timing wasn't right," I kept telling myself. Maybe it never will be. Maybe I should just sit down with her and tell her that I love her. Will she slap me in the face? Will she resent me for telling her how I feel or for not telling her sooner? Maybe she'll tell me she feels the exact same way. Is this a risk I'm willing to take?

Xander

I sit up as much as I can and focus on what the doctor says. I'm tired, my vision is blurred, and my mouth feels like I'm swallowing cotton balls. The inside of my mouth is covered in sores. A side effect of radiation to my head. I lick my dry lips, but there's nothing to moisten them.

My doctor says, "I have some good news: Your tumor has shrunk enough for us to do the surgery." Closing my eyes, I quietly thank God.

"We need to get your strength up and then we can operate."

"How soon?" Mom asks.

"I'm hopeful we can do it as early as next week."

I try to listen to the instructions the doctor gives us, but my mind isn't concentrating on that. It's concentrating on the possibility that I may have only one week to live. Seven days isn't enough time to spend with Ava. I know the surgery might work, but what if it doesn't? I have to make the next week count. Is this fair to Ava? I'm a selfish bastard for thinking only of my own needs. I think I love her and I need to be with her for as long as I can.

My book! I need to make some changes in my book. Wesley will understand. They're only some minor changes like maybe the title. *No, he'll never go for that.* The title has to stay, it's already up for pre-order. I do have some control over what goes *into* the book. It won't take long.

God knows I may not have long, and I'll be damned if I spend the next week with my nose in a computer.

On the drive home, Dad drives along the beach and we watch the wild horses run along the water's edge. I try to focus on the horses and the boats in the water. I don't care how many times I see this view, it never gets old. My vision is blurred and it makes it difficult to see.

"When you get your strength up, we should take the boat out, Xander," Mom says. "We can show Ava the true beauty of the Outer Banks."

I look at Ava and she smiles. I had planned on taking Ava out on my boat, but my plans didn't include my family. If my strength and vision don't return quickly, I'll have no other choice but to bring my family along with us.

"Sounds like a plan," I say.

When we get home, I nap. When I wake up, Ava isn't in the room with me. I use this time to my benefit. I call Wesley and update him on my health. Of course, Mom has already talked to him. I also tell him about the changes I need to make in the book. He doesn't argue with me like he has in the past.

He says, "Okay, I will make the changes for you, then send them over for your approval. Once you approve them, I'll get the proof copies of the paperback ordered."

"Today. Wesley, I need the corrections done today."

"I figured as much. You'll have them this evening."

"Thank you."

"Well, I think this book will be your number one best seller. If I can help make that happen for you, I want to be there for that."

"You're a good friend."

"That, and I'm greedy. We stand to make some serious money from this book."

When I get an uncontrolled cough, he says, "Get some rest and I'll take care of you on this end."

I can't say anything so I just disconnect the call. Ava and Mom are in the room immediately. They both look scared. Ava gets me some water and it helps. "Cotton mouth?" Ava asks. I just nod as I finish off the water. "We'll keep some water on the nightstand for you." I hand her the empty glass. "I'll get you some more."

"Thank you."

"Can I get you anything?" Mom asks.

"I don't need anything." I can see the fear in her eyes. "I didn't mean to frighten you."

She gives me a weak smile. "It's hard not to these days. It seems that everything about this is frightening."

I raise my arm for a hug. Mom hugs me tightly but gently. "In another week, all this may be behind us."

"That would be nice, wouldn't it. I'll finally have my Xander back. "

Ava comes into the room quietly and sets the glass of water on the nightstand. She doesn't say anything as she backs out of the room to give Mom and me some privacy. "It would. This time next year, we all should plan a family trip to Spain."

"Spain? We always talked about doing that when you boys graduated from high school." Mom smiles and she no longer looks as frightened as she did a few moments ago.

Drew went into the military right after high school. Shortly after he got injured, I was diagnosed with cancer.

"I think it's about time we make it happen."

"When you get better after your surgery, we'll start making plans for a trip to Spain."

Mom, Drew, Dad, and Ava sit in my bedroom while I lie in bed. I want to get up, but I just don't have the strength. We talk and laugh, and sometimes I sleep. When I wake up, they are still there talking as if I never dosed off.

Over the next few days, I can feel I'm getting stronger. The doctor stopped the oral chemo and radiation to give my body time to strengthen. I'm grateful for that, as the chemo is hard on my body. Ava, Drew, Dad, and Mom spend every minute of the day with me. At night, Ava and I stay up late talking.

"I'm glad you're feeling better."

I touch her soft hair. "Me, too. Just in time for the surgery."

"Well, you still have a couple more days. Is there anything you want to do?"

I think about the things I need to do before my surgery. Christmas is only a couple weeks away. I should probably do some Christmas shopping. Wesley called and said my proof copies of my book should arrive tomorrow. I'm excited about that. The book's completion is at the top of my priority list.

"On-line Christmas shopping would be nice," I finally say.

"That's easy enough. Do you have a list?"

I wanna laugh, but I don't. "I don't need a list. I have just a few people to buy for."

"That's even better."

I watch as she gets out my laptop and hands it to me to enter my passcode. It doesn't take long to shop for Mom, Dad, and Drew. I also shop for Skylar and Nichole.

"Do you need anything else?"

"I need to buy one more gift, but I'll do that when you're not in the room with me."

"Are you sure? 'Cause I think I can help you with that."

We both laugh. "Yeah, pretty sure I can do it alone."

"Okay, have it your way." She leans in and kisses me. "I need something to drink. Can I get you something?"

Of course my mouth is dry. "I'll take water, with lots of ice, please."

"Okay. I'll give you a few minutes. Don't go crazy shopping."

She waits for me to answer. "I won't." It's the truth. I already know what I want to get for her.

Chapter Four: A Final Goodbye or a Second Chance

Ava

The last week has been a whirlwind of emotions. One minute, Xander looked like death itself, and then the next, he was up eating and talking. If Xander is worried about his upcoming surgery tomorrow, I would never know. He never shows his fear.

He had a box delivered to him this week. Originally, I thought it was his Christmas gifts he bought this week, but I may have been wrong. I didn't get to see what was in the box, and he never showed me either. I didn't ask and he didn't tell me. He's entitled to his secrets.

When Xander feels well, we talk and he visits with his family. When he's sick, I lie in bed with him and read to him or try to memorize his facial features, the shape of his hands, and the smell of his scent. I try to match my rapid breathing to his shallow breaths.

I think back to the last few months I've had with Xander, and I smile. He's brought a lot of happiness into my life. He's funny, good looking, and talented, and he will and can do just about anything. After losing my memory to amnesia, I'm happy to say that I'm replacing any memory loss with new and improved ones. I have no idea what the future holds for Xander and me, but the last few months with him have been wonderful. He's everything a woman could ever want in a man.

"What are you smiling at?" he asks.

Surprised that he was watching me, I say, "You." I scoot back so I can get a better look at him. "I didn't know you were awake."

"I haven't been up long." He squeezes his eyes shut. "This headache woke me up."

"Do you want something for it?"

I watch as he licks his dry lips. "Yes, and something to drink."

Leaning up, I kiss him. "I'll be right back."

I go downstairs. Daniel, Drew, and Rachael are sitting around the dining room table.

"Hey, Xander has a headache. Is there anything for him to take?"

I get into the fridge and get him a bottle of cold water, while his mother gets me some Motrin. When we hear a thump coming from upstairs, we all run to see where the noise is coming from. Drew and Daniel are the first ones to arrive in Xander's bedroom.

"Call 911," Daniel yells.

My heart races as I search frantically search for my cell phone. It's in the bedroom lying on the nightstand.

Drew says, "He's having a seizure."

"I'll call 911, you help Xander," Rachael cries.

I rush into the room and see that Xander is having a grand mal seizure. My heart races and my mind replays the first time I learned he had cancer. With tears in my eyes, I try to do everything I know to do as a nurse for him. I whisper for him to come out of his seizure. When one seizure leaves, another seizure begins. After six seizures in a row, I give up hope that they'll stop on their own.

"Call his doctor," I cry from a kneeling position on the floor.

I do the only thing I can do for him: I pray, and keep him safe during his seizures. I don't think I breathe until I hear the sirens in the far distance.

Rachael brings everyone upstairs and the chaos increases. I update the EMS workers on what I know about today's seizures, and Rachael and Daniel update them on Xander's health problems and allergies.

We shuffle down the stairs and file into one car. Rachael rides in the ambulance with Xander. The ride to the hospital is a blur. His surgery was scheduled for tomorrow. How could this happen? I was just talking to him. This can't be the end. His tumor was shrinking; his doctor confirmed it. He'll recover from this, just like he did his last seizures. He'll have his surgery and everything will work out for him as it should. This is just a little setback.

"Ava? We should go."

I look up and for a minute, I'm confused. It looks like Xander standing in front of me holding his hand out for mine.

"We need to go, Ava." *It's Drew speaking, not Xander.*

Silently, I take Drew's hand and step out of the 4x4 truck. I walk behind Drew and Daniel. I say nothing. I have no words to say to anyone. This can't be happening. I feel small and helpless, and the sounds of a busy hospital are muffled. I can't make out what people are saying. Why can't I hear? Suddenly, I'm cold. Very cold. I try to warm my arms with my hands, but it's all in vain.

Rachael joins us in the waiting room. Her tear-stained cheeks say what her heart feels. She's broken. I look at Drew before I look at Daniel. Daniel is always the strong one in the family and he's torn. He's trying to be strong for his wife and son, but it's taking all he has. I want to step up and offer some strength, but I have nothing to offer.

Someone hugs me and it's welcoming. I have no idea who it is, but I let them.

"I came as soon as I knew the ambulance was there for Xander. Is there any news?" Nichole releases her hold on me.

I shake my head; I'm still unable to speak.

"We should sit, it could be awhile," Nichole says, sitting down.

I watch Nichole and it dawns on me that she was going through a similar situation a year ago when Connor and I were in the accident that took her son's life. *Is she reliving that night she lost her only child?*

She hugs everyone before we take a seat in the waiting room. The room is noisy, but none of the noise is coming from any of us. We sit quietly, in our own thoughts, and me in my own personal hell. *Did I push Xander to have the surgery? Did I tell him it would prolong his life? If this doesn't work out, am I to blame?*

The doctor comes out and calls us back. He says, "We have Xander stabilized, but he's still unconscious. The x-rays are showing there's another tumor, and it's pressing against his brain stem."

Rachael stumbles.

"What does this mean?" Daniel asks.

"It means we need to operate now."

"We can see him first, right?"

"Of course. The surgery will be in about another hour."

We follow the doctor to Xander's hospital room. His room isn't just an emergency treatment room; this room reminds me of an intensive care room. He's hooked up to more needles and machines than I could have imagined. Rachael cries. Either Xander will live, possibly with his brain and body no longer working correctly, or he'll die. I don't need to be reminded of the seriousness of this. These last few weeks have been tough on him; they've been tough on all of us. The nurses graciously provide enough chairs for everyone.

The mood is somber in the room. I knew Xander was having surgery tomorrow, but we would still have tonight together. I wasn't counting on our time being cut short. I had so many things I wanted to say to him, to tell him. I'll never be able to tell him with so people in the room.

Although Xander is unconscious, we all talk to him as if he's sitting up in the bed listening to us. Rachael tells him about their plans for Christmas, and about their next summer family vacation. Drew tells him as soon as he's up to it, they'll have to plan a boating/ fishing trip together. Daniel tells him that as soon as he's better, they're going to finish building that sailboat they started when he was in high school. I remind him that he still owes me a date and I'm waiting for it. It's not what I wanted to tell him, but there's a room full of people and I don't want to share my personal thoughts with anyone other than Xander.

When they come in to take Xander to surgery, we cry. We say our goodbyes, without making it sound like it's a forever goodbye. I kiss him and hold my cheek next to his. He's cold. I don't want him to go. I don't want him to have cancer. I wish this was just another one of my nightmares.

We're escorted into the surgery waiting room where the waiting nightmare begins. We make coffee, we cry, we pace, and we wait. I don't think anyone sleeps or rests.

Rachael taps her foot quickly and continuously. A nurse comes out and updates us several times throughout the surgery. So far, so good. As long as we get good news, I can wait.

When we haven't heard anything for a while, we all become concerned. A nurse enters the room and calls us back. *He must be out of surgery. Thank God.* We follow the nurse down a hall past the recovery rooms. *This isn't good.* Rachael holds on to the wall for support. The doctor is waiting for us when we walk into the room. Any hope I had leaves my body and I begin to cry. The doctor doesn't say anything right away; he doesn't need to. Xander's gone. He lost his battle with cancer. He didn't have a chance to say goodbye. I didn't have a chance to say goodbye.

"I'm sorry, but we did everything we could to save him."

It's the sound of Rachael's cries that force me to cover my own ears. My heart hurts for my own loss, but also for Rachael, Drew, and for Daniel's loss. They lost a son and a brother.

"He had a seizure during the operation and we weren't able to control it." The doctor clears his throat and says, "In a few minutes, you can go in and say your goodbyes." The doctor pauses again. "We'll need to know what the arrangements are for him."

Daniel wipes away his tears, "His wishes were to be cremated. Gallop Funeral Services will be in charge of the arrangements."

"Thank you. We'll make the call to their office."

We cry and try to console each other. Even Nichole cries. I'm not sure if she's crying for Xander, for his family, or for her own loss of her own son not long ago. *Xander was taken too soon. It's not fair. He had so much talent and love.* It's not right when a young person loses their life. It's not supposed to be like that. You're supposed to live to be old and die an old crabby person. Parents aren't supposed to bury their child. I wipe away the steady flow of tears as I remember happier times with Xander.

"I'll miss him. Xander brought happiness into my life during the short time I knew him." I cry some more. "He was always such a gentleman," I add.

The nurse lets Drew, Rachael, and Daniel go back and see Xander. Nichole and I wait in the private room. "I'm sorry I don't remember Connor. I know his death was extremely hard on you."

Nichole takes my hand. "Thank you, Ava. I'm sorry that Connor wasn't as good to you as he should have been, but I'm glad that you have Chase and had Xander in your life."

I smile at the thought of both of them. Even though Xander is gone, I'm very blessed to have known him. And Chase... he's just amazing.

"Me, too."

When it's my turn to see Xander, I walk slowly into the room. His lifeless body lies on the bed covered only with a thin sheet. Through blurred vision I force myself to take each step as I near him. The steady stream of tears races down my cheeks, staining my face. When I finally reach Xander, I realize the truth. This isn't a dream. Xander's gone and he's not ever coming back. I cry, I beg him to come back. I beg God to let him live. I promise to be better, to be nicer, to be kinder. I promise to go to church, to give weekly to the offerings, and to be a positive role model in every way. I promise to be and do all of these things if Xander can live. I know you're not supposed to barter with God, but people don't always think rationally at times like these. I'm not ready to say goodbye. I have so much I need to say to him. There's so much for us to do. It wasn't his time.

I don't curse God for taking him too soon. I don't question God and ask why. I sit beside Xander and kiss his cold hand. I tell him how much he meant to me, and how much I learned from him. I tell him that God brought him into my life at a perfect time, and I will be forever thankful for that. I tell him I don't know what I'll do without him. My days at the inn won't be the same without him. I won't have a good-looking man walk through the doors on a daily basis. I won't have someone help Skylar and me carry in the groceries, or help set up breakfast with me in the morning. I'll still have Skylar, but she isn't Xander.

Drew, Daniel, and Rachael walk into the room and I stand. I dry my eyes, but it's useless. The tears don't stop. I look at Drew and he looks so much like Xander. As long as I know Drew, I'll never have to wonder what Xander would look like as he aged. They walk slowly towards the bed. Daniel helps Rachael stand. I hug each of them and tell them how sorry I am for their loss. We cry and we hug. As sad as I am, I cannot begin to imagine their pain.

The ride home from the hospital is a somber one. Soft cries and sniffles fill the silent air. I want to be there for Xander's family. I want to help them through this difficult time. *They said his wishes were to be cremated. Will they have a memorial service for him? Will they have a ceremony where they spread his ashes someplace beautiful? Or is today the final goodbye?* I'll ask them about their plan later.

When we get to the house, Nichole is waiting for us on the front porch. She hugs everyone as they walk into the large foyer. When she hugs me she says, "Is there anything I can do?"

"I don't think so. You being here is a big help." *It's the truth.*

Rachael makes coffee, while Drew and Daniel shower. Are they trying to wash the events of the day off their bodies? *I might see if that works.* I walk up to Rachael as she's looking out the window at the ocean. Touching her arm gently I ask, "Are you all right?"

She dries her tears and offers a sad smile. "I loved him so much." Another tear falls.

I use the restroom and change Xander's sheets before joining the family in the kitchen. They have several photo albums out and are sharing happier times with each other. Drew laughs and says, "Ava won't be able to tell."

This sounds like a challenge. "Tell what?" I ask as I get Nichole and me a cup of coffee.

"Who is who," Rachael says, holding up two baby pictures.

I've never had a hard time telling Xander and Drew apart. I think I would know Xander anywhere, even in his younger years. "I bet I can." I smile. I want to keep the mood going. "Line up some photos for me." I add cream and sugar in my coffee before walking over to the table where Drew is just finishing setting some photos on the table of him and Xander from birth to adulthood. I look at Drew, Rachael, and Daniel who are all smiling, although their eyes are still laced with sadness. I focus my attention back on the photos. Setting my coffee cup down away from the pictures, I start sorting through them. The ones on the right are Xander, and the ones on the left are of Drew. There are only a couple of pictures I'm not completely sure about, but I think I'm mostly correct in identifying the twins.

"Done," I announce proudly.

I wait for someone to move some pictures around but no one does. Everyone laughs and it confirms that I can tell the identical twins apart even as newborns. "She did better than you did, Daniel." Rachael laughs softly. "I used to have to put different-colored socks on the boys when they were born so Daniel wouldn't get them mixed up."

"Really? I know they are identical, but I can tell a difference." *Xander is much better looking. Of course I keep that information to myself.* "Xander told me that the girls you dated in high school couldn't tell you two apart."

"They couldn't. We were idiots to date someone like that. Of course, back then, it was fun." Drew looks sad. "I'm gonna miss him. He was the best brother I ever could have had."

The happy mood turns somber. "He was pretty amazing."

"Thank you. He thought very highly of you, Ava," Daniel says.

I swallow the lump in my throat. "He helped me through a very hard time in my life."

"He went to Savannah when he found out his cancer had grown." *Wait? What?* "We think he went there to die." Tears fall when I listen to Daniel talk about Xander. *He went there to die? Did he give up all hope?* "He found you and found a new reason to live. The last few months were truly his happiest he's ever been and we owe that to you."

"Your son was easy to like. He was easy to be around." I smile with fondness. "I wish I had met him sooner, and had known him longer. Xander was pretty amazing."

"Thank you, Ava."

I brush away the tears. "Do you know if there will be a memorial service?"

Daniel and Rachael look at each other. "Xander didn't mention anything. He said he wanted to be cremated immediately. He didn't want his family mourning over his soulless body."

Daniel says, "That reminds me. I need to call Wesley so he can set up a press conference. Xander's readers will need to know of his passing. I mean of Jami Alexander's passing."

Drew says, "Once word leaks about his passing, people will be coming from everywhere to pay their respects for the famous author Jami Alexander."

"You're right," Nichole says. "I don't think you'll be able to hide his identity."

Daniel says, "We've always been pretty modest about Xander's writing, but in all reality, his book sales have been anything but modest."

I remember when I first learned that Xander was Jami. It was when Carla Jo Dean was in the tea room.

"He's a big deal for sure," I confirm.

The next morning, Daniel turns the television on CNN News. The headline reads, "*New York Times* Best-Selling Author Jami Alexander Loses Battle with Cancer."

Drew says, "Maybe they won't link Xander with Jami. He's done an excellent job hiding his identity."

Daniel says, "That's Wesley calling now."

My phone rings, it's Skylar. I stand and walk out of the room and say, "Hey, Skylar."

Skylar

"I just heard. Is it true that Xander died?"

"Yeah, it is."

"Are you all right?"

"I'm sad, we're all sad."

"Xander was a great guy, he'll be missed for sure."

"Yeah, he was and he will."

"Hey, I hate to bring this up, but have you seen the news?"

"We just turned it on, why?"

"Ava, your boyfriend's a rock star."

I can hear her laugh through the phone, "What do you mean?"

"He's trending today on social media. He's the most tweeted, and his new book is the most pre-ordered. He's everywhere. Everyone's talking about him, I mean her."

"Has anyone mentioned him at the inn?"

"No, not yet. It's just a matter of time."

"Can I call you back?"

"Sure."

He didn't want the guests to learn that Xander was the famous author Jami Alexander. Claire and I are still in mourning over his death, but we are in shock over the celebrity status the news is giving him.

"I have to wonder, when someone dies, do they automatically become more famous?"

"I don't think so. I think Xander was just down to earth, and it was hard to imagine his fame and fortune when someone is so much like us."

"His whole family is amazing. He'll surely be missed." I smile at the fond memories of Xander, Ava, and me.

"Are there any other authors in their family?" Claire asks.

I have to think. "I don't recall ever asking about it or Ava ever mentioning it. Maybe the dad, I'm not sure. Ava's the reader more than I am, she would know."

"I was just wondering."

Later that night, Claire and I are in the kitchen. "What are you in the mood for?" she asks.

Without hesitation I say, "Fried chicken, homemade noodles with white flour, mashed potatoes made with real butter, and blackberry pie with homemade crust." She laughs and I feel the need to clarify. "With Xander being sick and having to eat healthy, we didn't eat the foods I just mentioned. I would love nothing more than some fattening, Southern home cooking."

"It's obvious that you don't eat that unhealthy all the time, so I'd say, let's go for it."

"It's not nice to tease a hungry girl."

Looking around the kitchen she says, "I'll make the noodles; you go to the store and get some fryers and some fresh blackberries."

"You're serious?"

She opens some cabinets looking for something. "Yes, but you better hurry. A meal like this will take some time to make."

Running to get my purse and my car keys, I say, "Claire, I freaking love you."

I run through the store grabbing junk food I've craved, but refused to buy. Caramel squares, Hershey's candy bars, chocolate-covered cherries. I also buy the fresh berries and fryers Claire asked for. Of course, berries are one of the healthiest foods you can eat, so maybe I should eat two slices of berry pie. I add a few bags of chips and pretzels to complete my carb purchase. If I binge eat on carbs, I should do it right. I have only until Ava gets home to eat all the junk food I can. She eats healthy and wants everyone around her to as well. I get that, and I try to follow her example, but I'm not disciplined like Ava. I need my sweets and salty food sometimes. I need my adult beverages sometimes, too. Maybe more than one. *Wine, I need wine.* If the choice is between no wine plus a perfect weight versus wine plus five pounds overweight, I choose wine plus five pounds overweight. I shop for wine before checking out.

I rush home where Claire is making homemade egg noodles. I unload my groceries on the counter where she smiles at my unorthodox purchase. It's unusual to some, but to me, it was a perfect shopping trip. I open some wine and pour us each a glass. I also open a bag of pretzels to snack on while we cook. I play a little Christmas music as I start to wash the berries for the pie. We talk about Ava and wonder when she'll be home. I also talk about Xander and how sad we are at losing him. Between washing the berries and cleaning the chicken, I text Drew.

Skylar: *Just thinking about you. I am so heartbroken over your loss. Xander was a great guy and he will be missed. I hope you and your family are doing okay under the circumstances.*

Drew: *Thank you. It'll take time, but I think we'll be okay.*

I think about calling him, but then I don't want to bother him and his family. I know they are grieving.

While making dinner, Claire and I drink wine and sing along to the Christmas carols on the radio. It's a temporary fix of feeling the devastating loss of Xander. It isn't until I go to bed that I have time to let his death sink into my soul. He's never coming back. Xander will never walk through those doors again. It's a sad truth. I honestly believed that he would be okay. My focus is now on Ava. Will she be okay? How will she deal with his loss? I want to call her but it's late.

Skylar: *Just lying here thinking about you.*

Ava: *Everything smells of him.*

Skylar: *You're in his bed?*

Ava: *I wanted to be close to him.*

Skylar: *I'm sorry.*

Ava: *Thank you.*

Skylar: *Try to get some sleep. Xoxo*

Ava: *Goodnight. Xoxo*

Claire and I work well together, but I miss Ava. When she and Drew pull up into the driveway during the afternoon tea, I'm thrilled. I leave Claire and run to the door. I'm not sure whom I'm happier to see: Ava or Drew. It's Ava, of course. They both look sad and I rush over to Ava first as I smile at Drew as I walk past him. If he's any kind of a man, he'll understand my bond with my best friend. I hug her and kiss her on her cheek. She cries into my shirt and I let her. I smooth her long dark hair out of the way and speak softly into her ear. "It's all right." I hear the screen door shut and I know Claire is right behind me. She says something to Drew, and I feel better knowing someone is there for him. I slowly release my hold on Ava.

"You're back early," I say.

"I know. I needed to get back." She wipes away her tears. "Xander was cremated and his memorial service is still being worked out."

I nod my understanding. "I'm glad you're home."

"Me, too."

I turn to Drew and he looks devastated. "I'm so sorry." I hug him and he holds me tightly. "I've missed you." I nestle my face in the crook of his neck and inhale. He smells of ocean and fresh air.

"Oh, babe, I've missed you more."

"Are you okay?" I cry. *Why am I crying? He just lost his brother. He should be the one crying.*

"I will be."

"I'm so sorry." I want to say something worth hearing, but I have nothing. I don't know what to say to him. "He was a great man."

"Thank you, he was."

He doesn't release his hold and I don't care. I could stay in his strong arms forever. I want to comfort him, but I feel like he's comforting me. "How's your mom and dad?"

"Mom hasn't stopped crying. I'm actually glad Nichole is there with her. When we left, they were looking through photo albums, school yearbooks, and any other embarrassing report cards or ribbons he earned from pre-school until now."

I pull away and look at him since it's been awhile since I've seen him. "You shaved your head. It looks nice." *It's not a lie.* Not many people look good with a completely bald head, but Drew is one of the few people who do. His skull is perfectly symmetrical.

"Xander lost his hair from the aggressive chemo treatments. Dad and I shaved our heads to support him." A lump forms in my throat. He kisses my forehead and runs his hands up and down my arm. "We should get you inside, it's chilly out here."

I finish up the tea while Claire fixes Drew and Ava some lunch. Ava looks thinner than usual. I know this last week has been especially stressful on her, not to mention the last few days.

As soon as the tea is over, I hurry into our private living quarters. "There she is, let's see if she can tell," Ava says.

She must be talking about me. "Tell what?" I ask, walking toward the dining room table.

"I have faith that Skylar can pick her man out of a lineup," Drew says confidently.

Tell 'em, Babe. "I'll know Drew anywhere," I confirm without a doubt. *That's a lie. If it's Drew as an adult, I'm good. But if it's baby pictures, I'm screwed. I think all babies look alike.*

As I get closer I see several baby pictures sitting on the table of two babies who look identical. Ava smiles. She knows I think that all babies look alike. "Go ahead and pick out your man," she teases.

Drew stands tall and proud. I'm hoping to not disappoint him.

"You were able to pick out Xander, weren't you?"

She nods, "Yeah, in all 12 photos. This will be easy for you. There's only a few photos here for you to pick from."

She knows I can't do it. She's setting me up. I lean in and study the photos. I have no idea. I look hard, still nothing. Closing my eyes, I take a lucky guess. "He's the baby in the blue socks."

"High five, Babe. I knew you could do it." I smile, and high five Drew, while smiling back at Ava. *Go, me! I just hope he never finds out I had no idea which baby he was.*

"I knew you wouldn't let me down."

Later, when Ava and I put the food away, she asks, "You had no idea which baby Drew was, did you?"

I close the refrigerator door and say, "Not a clue."

"I didn't think so."

Ava

Lying in bed, I cry. Xander was taken too soon. His life wasn't over. It couldn't have been. He was young, too young. I look at the unfinished chess game we just started to play a week or two earlier. I smile at the memory. He was amazing and an incredible man. I didn't love him, but I liked him. Could I have loved him? I think so. He was easy to like. He was easy to spend time with. Honestly, I could have easily fallen in love with him.

I knew him for only a few short months, and I have only fond memories of him. Not one argument. Not one disagreement. Nothing but happy times, well, up until the last week. Conversations replay in my mind. Drew said he came to Savannah right after he learned his tumor had grown. *Lost in Savannah.* I get online and order his new book. It's been available for pre-order for only a few days and it's ranking number one in all categories. I decide to search other online retailers and he's ranking on all of those sites, too. I knew his books have always sold well, but I never looked to see how well. I knew Jami Alexander on a personal level. I smile at that. The bad things that have happened in my life have brought me here. To Savannah. To the inn. To Xander. I guess God did have a plan. I decide to order several paperback copies of his last book. *His last book.* It's sad to think about.

I close my laptop and cuddle into the pillow that Xander last used. I'm disappointed when his scent is faint. Soon there won't be anything left. My mind wonders about death and heaven. Can Xander see me? Does he know the pain I'm feeling? Is he with his parents and Drew? Is he in heaven studying some student handbook on *How To Be a Guardian Angel*? Or eating Mallo Cups by the six-packs? I'd like to think so. Has his vision returned to normal? Can he see Earth from Heaven?

Over the next week, the mood at the inn is somber for us, but we try to make it festive for our guests. We play Christmas music beginning at breakfast and it plays throughout the day and into the evening. The guests talk excitedly about their plans for the day, and Skylar and I try to not show our sadness.

Some days, I feel like we're just going through the motions. Skylar and I have breakfast with the guests and steer them in the direction of the best holiday festivities in town.

This morning, Drew and Skylar leave right after breakfast to finish up their Christmas shopping. Mom and I stay in and do some online shopping of our own.

"Mom, you know you can go home. You don't have to stay here with me."

"I know. It's your Dad's idea. He doesn't want you to be alone."

I look around the large house and when it's full of guests, it's hard to be lonely. "Will he be here for Christmas?"

"He will. He'd like to continue our Christmas Eve tradition."

When I was a child, we always had a big party on Christmas Eve. It was the highlight of the holiday season.

"I don't know if I'm up to it this year. So much sadness has happened to so many people we love and care about." I stop and my mind rushes with all of the bad things that have happened. This hasn't been the best year for me. I give Mom an example of why my mood is solemn. Not that she needs to be reminded of any of these events. "Look at what happened to Nichole this year."

"I know. But look at the good that came from it. She's finally free of that monster, and she's getting better every day." *That's true, she is.* "But what about Xander? It's just been a few days since his passing. I'm not sure I'm up to a big celebration."

"I understand. We can have dinner — just us. We still have to eat."

That's true, we do. Most memorial services end with a meal. Someone dies, we mourn, and then we return to living our lives. That's the way it's supposed to be. "Thank you for understanding."

On December 23, the last guest checks out of the house. The next guest doesn't check in until New Year's Eve. Apparently, Savannah has a big New Year's Eve celebration down by the water. I shouldn't be surprised. If there's a reason to celebrate, this town will do it in style.

By noon, the house is empty. The cleaners are gone, and I anticipate that Drew will be leaving to join his mom and dad for the holidays sometime today. I haven't asked Skylar about her plans, but I wouldn't be surprised if she goes back with him. I walk around the house, talking myself out of the depression that threatens to take my body hostage.

This is the time of day that we serve the afternoon tea. The tearoom is empty and I'm feeling sorry for myself. I hate that now, I'm second guessing my decision to buy the bed and breakfast and bring my dear friend, Skylar, into it with me. I should have made sure I was more stable than I was in my decision making. I laugh to myself. *She's a nut to have followed an amnesiac to another state to start a new business. Who in their right mind would do that?* A best friend, that's who. *Okay, Xander, I get it. Many blessings, I know. I can clearly see them. Is this how it's going to be? I feel sorry for myself, and Xander shows me what I have to be thankful for?*

Skylar and Mom walk into the room and Mom asks, "What are you smiling at?"

"Just thinking of Xander." *Although he's gone, he's still everywhere.* "Do you think it's too late to have a Christmas Eve party?"

"You want to do our traditional party now?" Mom asks.

"I know it's short notice, but yeah, I do. It won't seem like the holidays without our family and friends." I look around the big empty house. "Seems like such a waste to have the house empty for Christmas."

"No, it's never too late," Skylar says excitedly.

Just at that time the door opens and in walk Drew, Nichole, Rachael, and Daniel. I look at Skylar and whisper, "You already planned a party, didn't you?"

"It's my house, too. I thought it would be nice to do something with everyone. Besides, Chase didn't have anyplace to go. His parents went skiing in Colorado, and he was home for the holidays."

"You know I love you, right?" I hug Skylar and I am so thankful that I have her.

"Yeah, I know."

"Your dad and Chase should be here soon," Mom says.

As Skylar walks over to the door to help Nichole, Drew, and his family, she calls over her shoulder, "Mom and my brother Mark are coming, too."

I swear I think my heart does a happy dance.

"Good thing you have a house big enough to accommodate everyone," Mom giggles.

"No kidding. I think this will about fill up all of the rooms." I lean into her for a hug. "Thank you. I think this is just what I needed."

"Don't thank me yet, we still need to get groceries."

The day is filled with the arrival of our family. I make a list of the things we need from the store and Skylar and Drew entertain everyone with their short and sweet romance. I have no idea how serious it is, but if she's happy, that's all I care about. He's a good guy, and I know he'll be good to her. At least I hope he'll be good to her.

I am more than excited to see Dad and Chase. I've missed them both terribly. I hug Dad before I hug Chase. "It's been too long," I say to Chase.

"It has."

Once everyone is finally here and unpacked, we ease into a comfortable gathering. Some of the guys play Call of Duty on the big screen. Chase and Drew started a fire outside in the garden. Mom, Rachael, Jessica, and Nichole are baking, and everyone else is having spiked eggnog. The house is filled with laughter and it feels nice. Rachael, Daniel, and Drew look sad, but they're engaging in conversation and activities with others. I think this was a good idea. At least maybe their mind isn't fully on Xander's absence.

"Ava, before I leave this weekend, I'd like to speak with you in private." Dad is standing beside me.

"Sure, I have some time now."

He looks around the room and says, "Maybe later. It's not important, but we need to talk." He smiles, but it doesn't reach his eyes.

"Okay. Well, whenever you're ready, I'll be here."

Dad looks outside through the large picture window. "Do you want to sit outside by the fire?"

"Sure, I need a refill first."

I refill my glass and fill his glass before walking out into the chilly air. The fire warms me quickly. Nichole, Chase, Dad, and I are the only ones outside. It almost seems like we walked in on a business meeting. Chase and Nichole both smile. If it is a business meeting, it must be going in Nichole's favor.

"Are we interrupting?"

"Don't be silly," Nichole says. "It's getting chilly out here. I'll meet everyone inside." She stands and we watch her walk into the house.

"Did we interrupt?" I ask again.

"No, we were done."

"She's looking much better," I admit.

Chase smiles, "She is. She has good things coming her way in the new year."

That must mean about her divorce. I won't pry, but I want to ask what he means.

"She deserves it," Dad says.

Does he know something I don't know? I'll ask him later.

"She's been through a lot." Chase looks down at me. "How are you doing?"

"I'm good. Feeling pretty blessed today."

Chase runs his hands up and down his jeans-clad leg. "Me, too."

"Marshall, can you help?" Mom calls from the door.

"Coming, dear." He hollers over his shoulder, "See ya."

Once he's inside, Chase asks, "So, how are you really?"

He knows me so well. "I'll be okay. I'm sad. Death is sad. Xander was a nice guy, and it's not fair it happened to him."

"No, it isn't. Life isn't fair." He looks at the hot embers of the fire. "I think what we can do is learn from Xander."

"What do you mean?"

"He lived well. He had a good life. He treated others with respect. I imagine his life was fulfilled and mostly complete prior to his death. Not everyone can get a grasp on life like he did. Although he was taken sooner than he should have, he lived his life better than most."

"That's a pretty good analysis."

"Thanks. I'm an attorney. It's my job to know people and know the types of people they are."

"You know just before he died he finished his last book."

He looks at me sadly. "I heard. Girls in the office were talking about pre-ordering it. They're quite sad over the loss of Jami Alexander."

I have to wonder what his thoughts are on me. No better way to know than to ask. "What about me? Do you think I'm wasting my life doing nothing?"

He furrows his brow. "No, not at all. Any amnesiac who packs up and moves to another state to start her life over, while chasing her dreams, is doing anything but wasting her life."

I smile. I never looked at myself like that. "I did that, didn't I?"

"You did that, and you're still doing that, Ava. You're amazing and I'm incredibly proud of you."

I blush. "Thank you. I appreciate that."

"You're welcome." He watches as the fire dies down. "Should I add another log or are you ready to go inside?"

"Although I would love to stay outside, I think we should go in."

"Yeah, you're probably right."

When we walk inside, I can see Nichole on the phone in the other room. I sit at the table with Rachael and Daniel. They are very grateful for being out of the house for Christmas. I share with them what Chase said about Xander living life to the fullest. They both shed tears, but they are happy tears. I thought it was worth sharing and worth hearing again.

We all engage in teams of charades, Scrabble, and Pictionary. I suck at them all, but I don't care. It's the most fun I've had in a long time. Mark and Skylar are on teams and there is no beating them at anything. Something tells me I should have known this about them from the beginning. After too many to count high-fives and fist bumps from the Sperry family, my team loses. Later we are joined by everyone else, until Mark and Skylar are the last two standing. Everyone in the house laughs as the two declare themselves to be the unbeatable winners.

I tell the others, "The first time I played charades, I was in middle school, taking beginning piano lessons. The word I chose was Mozart, but no one guessed my word because I made a mistake. I indicated that my word was pronounced with three syllables, but it is pronounced with two. I was wrong when I thought it was pronounced 'Moe-te-zart.'"

Chase says, "A cousin of mine is named Bruce Bruce, believe it or not. He was named by a practical joker who thought that Bruce was a nice name; now he goes by his middle name: David. While playing charades, a friend of his indicated that her phrase was two words, and then she pointed twice to a bruise on her leg. Bruise bruise? Oh, Bruce Bruce!"

We all pitch in with the cleanup and say our goodnights for the evening. Skylar walks around with me and makes sure everything is locked up.

"Sweet dreams, Ava," Chase says, standing at my bedroom door.

"Goodnight, Chase. I'll see you in the morning."

"Okay." He turns to leave before turning back around. I follow his eyes to the chess game sitting on the table in the corner of the room. "You're playing?"

"Xander and I started a game." I get sad, thinking we'll never finish it. "Do you play?" I ask hopefully. If I had my memory, I would know the answer.

"Who do you think bought you that set?"

"You did?"

"Of course. You needed some practice with your pathetic playing skills."

"Pathetic?"

He tries hard not to laugh. "The truth hurts … sorry."

"Care to see how my skills have… improved?" I hold the door open wide for him to enter.

He cracks his knuckles and walks into my bedroom. "You don't still cry like a girl when you lose, do you?"

I throw my head back and laugh more than necessary. "Game on, Murphy."

"Murphy? Trying to intimidate me by using my last name?" He walks further into the room. "Emerson, it'll take more than that to scare this champ!"

We sit at the table and look at the game already in process. Chase sits in the same seat Xander was sitting at. We each have two pawns and one bishop off the table. I don't have the heart to start Xander's game all over.

"Looks like Xander was a great player, I can live with this. Whose turn was it?"

I remove the marker from the table and say, "My move."

"Of course it is."

Chase

Ava's gotten much better at chess than I remember. Of course, I don't tell her that. She's a lot cockier than I remember, too. It's cute and fun to watch.

When Ava yawns, I finish my move and stand to leave. "Looks like you'll have to wait until tomorrow to wallow in self pity."

She yawns again. "You're leaving? I'm just about ready to attack with my queen."

I pull her chair out for her. "Come on, Queenie. You'll have to save your queen for tomorrow, For tonight, it's lights out for you." She shuffles into the bathroom and comes out wearing a tee-shirt and shorts. I hold the covers up for her to crawl into bed. "Goodnight, Ava." I bend down and kiss her on her forehead. I leave my mouth there longer than I intended to. I've always had a special place in my heart for Ava. I inhale one last time before standing to leave. "Sweet dreams."

"Chase?"

"Yes, Ava?"

She turns on her side. "Thank you for everything. Not just for tonight, but for the things I can't remember you've done for me."

She never has to thank me for anything. "It's always my pleasure." I turn off her lamp before closing the door tightly. I can't think of one thing that I wouldn't do for her.

I walk upstairs to my room and notice that Nichole's door is open and her light is on. I knock gently.

"Come in."

I open her door and stand in the doorway. "Still up?"

"I am. Too excited to sleep."

She's sitting on her bed with her laptop opened. "Is that it?"

"It is."

She turns her laptop around for me to see. I scan each image and I smile my approval. "Very nice."

"We have an appointment at 10:00 am." She looks again at the images on the computer screen. "Are you sure you don't mind? You've done so much for me already."

"Nichole, I'm thrilled to be able to help you with this next chapter in your life. I spoke to Marshall and he also wants to go with us. I hope that's okay."

"Oh, that's wonderful. I'd love to have another set of eyes. Thank you. What a great idea."

"I'm heading to bed. I'll see you in the morning."

"Goodnight, Chase."

I shower before bed, because in the morning it won't do me any good. Nichole, Marshall, and I are on a mission, and it'll be a dirty one. I toss and turn, not sure if I slept at all. The smell of coffee is welcoming. It lets me know I can soon get my caffeine fix, and that others in the house are up. I dress in jeans, a flannel shirt, and a pair of tan Timberlands before making my way to the kitchen. I assumed I would be one of the first few up, but I was wrong. Every guy in the house is already dressed and sitting at the kitchen table. "Mornin'." *Maybe I did sleep last night.*

I walk past them to the coffee pot where Jessica, Claire, Rachael, and Nichole are standing. I fill my mug with hot coffee and Marshall says, "We have a small problem."

I have no idea what he can be talking about. The only *problem* that I can think of is Brett, and I know he isn't a problem. "I'm listening."

"The girls all want to go and look at Nichole's possible new business." And right on cue, here come Skylar and Ava from their separate bedrooms.

Skylar says, "Yep, we want to see it, too."

I look at Nichole, "I thought you wanted to keep it a secret?" *Women and their secrets.*

She laughs and bares a huge smile. "I had to tell someone. Rachael, Drew, and Daniel are also coming."

"That's fine." I look at Skylar and Ava. "I want you to understand that it isn't open for business. What you have imagined in your head for a bakery isn't what you'll be seeing today."

"We know. Remember this place when we looked at it."

How could I forget. "Okay. Just didn't want you to have unrealistic expectations."

They are both dressed as if they'll be crawling in a basement. Ava slips her foot into a boot. "We won't."

We get ready and I'm surprised at everyone who wants to go and show their support for Nichole. We take three cars and head out to the location where Nichole instructed us to go. When we arrive, there is one Realtor there to show us, all of us, the property. When three carloads full of people pull up, I feel bad for the guy.

Marshall, Drew, Mark, and Daniel take off and walk around the building, while Nichole and I and the others stay and listen to his sales pitch. He opens the door to the bakery first, then the door leading upstairs to the apartment next. Skylar and Ava take off for the stairs while everyone else roams around the bakery. It actually looks better than I thought it would. The building comes equipped with the ovens, refrigerators, industrial appliances, the display cabinets and shelves, and the serving dishes. Everything seems to be in working order. The bakery is even large enough for two-top and four-top tables.

I check the pipes and the plumbing, and Nichole checks the lighting and the windows. When we go upstairs, Skylar and Ava are coming down the stairs. They don't give us any idea of their opinion of the upstairs apartment. That has me concerned. *Girls are usually giddy when they like something. Aren't they?*

The upstairs is open and airy. Large windows, beautiful hardwood floors, granite counters, Spanish-style light fixtures, and stainless steel appliances.

"Wow, I didn't see this coming," I say honestly.

Nichole remains quiet and walks into each of the bedrooms. "Two bedrooms with walk-in closets *and* they each have an ensuite bathroom," she says louder than necessary.

"I know," Ava yells from downstairs.

We all laugh. I leave and meet the guys outside. I want to see the structure of the building before Nichole signs off on the loan papers. I'm pretty sure if she has her way, this place is already sold.

The guys and I all agree the structure of the building is sound and the asking price seems fair. It seems like a good deal, but I'm glad it's a holiday so Nichole will have some time to think about it. I know the apartment alone is enough to make me want to put a bid in it just for myself.

Once we're done here, we head back to the inn. The Christmas party begins this evening at 5:00 and I still have a few things I need to do. I take everyone home and head out to do some last-minute shopping.

Ava

I'm so happy to see Nichole excited about something. I may be even more excited knowing she might be moving to Savannah. It might be selfish on my part. I can't help it. I like her and sometimes I think of how much I miss my family and the few friends whom I know.

"Are you already making mental plans of what you'll do with it?" I ask.

She giggles. "No, you heard Chase. He said to think about it."

"Making plans is thinking about it, isn't it?"

Skylar interrupts, "Sure is. I'd give it a fresh coat of paint, and call it home."

"You would. There's so much to think about? Taxes, insurance, parking, hours of operation. How much staff will be needed to run it?" I put the ham in the oven and set the timer.

"There's a lot to consider. That's for sure." Nichole looks worried.

"I'm not saying you can't make it happen. I think with the right staff, you'll have one heck of a successful business."

"Thank you, Ava. You've always been so kind and sweet."

"It's true, Nichole. If I can help you in anyway, let me know."

"I will. I just need to make a smart decision. Being new to the area and not knowing anyone will make it difficult to find staff to work for me."

"We did it," Skylar says.

We prepare the food and get the house ready for the party. The house feels and smells like Christmas. Cranberry candles are burning in every room, electric candles are plugged in and glowing in every window, the Christmas lights outside are lit, and music is playing from inside the foyer.

I look at the clock and it's almost 5:00. Chase isn't home yet, and I begin to worry. I walk into the kitchen and everyone is either busy preparing food, or they're busy fixing their drinks. I just watch the interaction of our combined families and I feel extremely blessed to be a part of such an amazing group of people. I watch Rachael, Daniel, Drew, and Skylar. They're laughing and seem to be having a good time. They seem to have accepted Skylar with open arms, which makes me feel good. She's an amazing person, and she and Drew seem to get along so well. Drew looks over at me and flashes me a perfect smile that makes me think of Xander.

"Am I late?" a voice asks in a whisper. It's Chase.

Looking at my watch, I say, "You're just in time." Since everyone is here, I can now enjoy the party. I pour a glass of wine and walk around and mingle listening to a little of everyone's conversations.

I can't remember my past, but something about this evening is very familiar. Everyone is dressed up in dresses and suits and ties. Something unsettling comes over me giving me the feeling of doom. I hate when this happens. This mostly happens in my sleep in the form of night terrors. I shiver from the cold chills that now freeze me from the inside out.

I focus my attention on my family and friends. At least in my waking hours, I can control the thoughts that try to consume my mind. Dad sees me and walks over to join me on the far side of the room. Chase smiles at me from across the room and it warms me.

"Are you having a good time?" Dad asks.

"I am. Everyone I love is gathered here in celebration. It's a lot to be thankful for."

"It is. This year brought new people into our lives."

Looking at Drew and his family, I smile. "I'm grateful for that."

When Chase joins us, Dad asks, "Let's eat, shall we?"

We sit around the large dining room table with the food set out in front of us. After Mark says the blessing, we eat. Laughter fills the air with stories of past Christmas mishaps, holidays gone wrong, and family bloopers. It's nice to laugh and know that not every family is perfect.

Jessica shares a story of when she was a small child. It was Christmas Eve and she and her brother got up to see if Santa Claus came yet. She says, "Under the tree was a pedal-powered, red fire engine truck for her brother. It said 'Fire Chief' across each side in white letters. It even had wooden ladders and a bell. I knew right then that Santa Claus was real because our parents didn't have that kind of money." She smiles and the memory. "I think it was the best Christmas ever."

Drew says, "I remember that one year Xander and I got almost identical bikes for Christmas." He laughs and says, "Imagine that." His dad laughs and clears his throat. "Sorry. Anyway, one was blue and one was red. I always got everything blue, but that year, I cried and cried because that was year I wanted the red one."

I remember Rachael saying she had to dress the twins in colored socks when they were born so Daniel could tell which child was which. Then yesterday, Skylar picked out Drew in the baby photos from the blue socks he wore in every picture. I glance up at him and he's wearing a navy blue tie. I guess the color blue has stuck with him.

Chase shares a story about when he was in college. He needed some extra money during Christmas so he got a job playing Santa Claus at Macy's Department Store. "On the first day of my job, I got dressed in my Santa suit and went to work. Never being around kids, I really never knew what to expect."

"I would love being around kids all day long," I say excitedly. I can only imagine how amazing it was for him.

"Would you?" he asks. "Let me recall my glorious experience with you. The first child kicked me. One child wiped a boogie on my sleeve. And let's not forget about the little girl who sneezed in my face."

"No!" I laugh.

"Oh, yeah. Flying snot and all."

"That's gross," Skylar laughs.

"Yeah, it was. The vomit was worse."

"She vomited, too?" I ask.

"No, I did."

Thankful his story came at the end of dinner. We have dessert and coffee as we talk about this holiday. "I didn't know what to get everyone for Christmas this year, so I decided on a group gift," Chase says.

Marshall says, "Chase, you didn't have to get anyone anything."

"I wanted to. When I saw it, I thought it was appropriate." He pulls out a picture from his back pocket and sets it in the center of the table. "I bought a tree that'll be planted in Xander's memory outside of Carla Jo Dean's Restaurant." He pauses for a moment. "I stand corrected, it'll be in Jami Alexander's memory." He explains that Skylar told him about the books Xander got from Carla Jo Dean and about meeting her for the first time. "She's a big fan of Jami's and is more than happy to have a tree planted in his memory."

"You did this today?" Rachael asks.

"It's been in the works for a few days. The tree and the plaque." He points to the oak tree and plaque in the photo and says, "I bought this today."

"Chase, I don't know what to say," Daniel says.

"You don't need to say anything. Carla Jo Dean would like to have a small memorial in the spring when the tree is planted. I know Xander's identity is a secret, but maybe we all could plan to attend that as a fan. She said she'll be in touch with a date."

"Man, this is really something," Drew says. "To have some big personality like Carla Jo Dean want to pay a tribute to Xander."

"He was a big deal," I say. I'm not talking about his author status either.

Rachael stands to hug Chase. "Thank you. It's nice to know that there'll be a place we can go to remember our son."

"You're welcome."

We pass the photo of the tree and the plaque around the table. It's totally unexpected and a pleasant surprise.

Nichole says, "I also have an announcement. It's not as big as Chase's, but it's exciting to me."

"You made an offer on the bakery?" I tease.

"I did and they accepted."

Wait? What? "I was only kidding."

"I loved it, and I have so many plans for it. I couldn't wait until after Christmas to make an offer. As soon as Chase and the guys confirmed the building was solid, I called the Realtor and made an offer."

"And they accepted?" Chase asked.

"And they accepted," she squeals.

"Looks like this calls for some champagne," Dad says, standing to walk into the kitchen.

We stand from the table and take the celebration into the other room. I hug Rachael, Daniel, and Drew. I also hug Chase and thank him for being an amazing guy. As the evening goes on and the celebration continues, Rachael takes me by the hand and leads me to the other room where the Christmas tree is sitting in the center of the large picture window. "We have something to give you, but we didn't want to do it with everyone watching."

I look from her to Daniel. "I have something for you guys, too."

"Ava, this isn't from us, it's from Xander."

My heart skips a beat. Holding onto the wall for support, I say, "Oh."

Daniel helps me to the couch where I sit gingerly. I watch as he goes to the tree and removes two packages. "Do you want to be alone?"

I don't know, do I? "I think I do."

"We understand." He places two gifts on my lap. The gift tags are written in Xander's handwriting. Gently, I trail my shaky fingers over the words. Someone pats my shoulder, but I have no idea who. When I hear the pocket doors close, I know I'm alone. I open the smaller gift on top first. Careful to not rip the paper, I remove the tape from one side of the package at a time. With shaky hands and tears in my eyes, I remove the lid to the box. Tucked inside is a handwritten note from Xander.

Ava,

If you're opening this, it means that I didn't survive the cancer. Don't cry. I had an amazing life and the last few months with you were nothing less than amazing. Probably the best in my entire life. My only regret is, I didn't have more time with you. This gift is to remind you that life goes on and it stops for nothing. Don't wait for tomorrow, it may never come.

Thank you for sharing your life with me. It made my life worth living.

Xander

When the tears stop, I remove the cotton that's protecting the gift, revealing a sterling silver infinity bracelet. *Infinity, life goes on and on.* I put it on and admire it. It's simple and beautiful. Removing the remnants of this gift, I focus on the next, larger gift. This gift tag isn't written in Xander's handwriting. Taking a deep breath, I just as carefully remove the wrapping paper. This gift isn't inside a box. I'm excited and surprised to see the gift is Jami Alexander's not-yet published book, *Lost in Savannah.* I've never had the opportunity to read a book from an author prior to being published before. This alone is pretty exciting. I hold it and admire the stunning cover as I realize that the image used is of my bed and breakfast. Xander took a photo of Rose Bud Inn and used it for his own book cover. I had no idea. I turn it over and read the blurb before opening it up and reading the inside flap. The book is signed and addressed to me. It reads:

Ava,

The sad truth is, I came to Savannah to die, but instead, I lived more in those few months than I have my entire life. Ava, my wish for you is to be happy. Find your passion and follow your heart. I want you to live your life the happiest you can possibly be. To forget the past and to seek an amazing future. Sometimes, happiness is standing right in front of you.

When you read this book, I think you'll see some resemblance to the woman who stole my heart.

You will always be the only one for me.

Love always, Xander

Chapter Five: A New Year

Ava

Christmas was wonderful. It came and went too fast in my opinion. Just before everyone leaves, I remember that Dad said he wanted to talk to me.

"Hey, we didn't get to talk."

"That's okay, it can wait until the next time."

"Are you sure? I have some time now."

"I'm sure."

He wanted to talk to me in private, it sounded like it was important. "Okay, whatever you say."

I kiss and hug Mom and Dad before they leave. Walking into the house, I sigh. "It's great having company, but wow, that was a lot of people."

"It was. I'm glad to have a few days of doing nothing before the guests start to arrive."

"Me, too."

"When is Drew coming back?"

"In a week or two. I needed some space. Things with him are great, but they're just moving so fast."

"They are, aren't they?"

"I like him. He's wonderful in every way, but so much has happened in such a short time." She stares up at the ceiling. "I just want some time to think."

"I get it. Go down to Tybee Island and spend the day."

"Do you want to come with me?"

"I think I'll pass. I want to read Xander's new book."

"Do you want me to stay around here? It sounds like that book is going to be a tear jerker."

That's putting it mildly. "No, I'll be fine."

As soon as Skylar's gone, I lock up the inn and lie on my bed and read. This book is written differently from Xander's other books. This could be a biography. It begins when his cancer is confirmed growing and spreading and when the doctor tells him he will die within the year without aggressive treatments and surgery. He writes about walking into the inn and seeing me for the first time. This book is written in first person and he describes his rapidly beating heart and his thoughts of seeing the most beautiful woman in the world. I cry. He changed the names of the characters, but he described them perfectly to our true appearance. He also used the real name of the inn and the tearoom.

To read about Xander's inner thoughts is private and personal. I had no idea what his first thoughts were of me. I read a little, and then I cry a lot. I don't stop reading until the book is finished. The book is amazing. Xander said in the book that he was madly in love with the innkeeper. Everything about the book was about our short life together. Did he really love me? He never said those words if he did. I often wondered if I loved him. I miss him, and I wanted more time with him. He loved me. He wanted me happy.

Setting the book down on the nightstand, I cry myself to sleep.

Standing in the corner of the room, I focus on the vision before me. A man who looks like every picture I have ever seen of Connor saunters across the room toward me. He's wearing a black suit, with a red tie. His hands are in his pockets, and he's sexy and handsome. His smile reveals straight white teeth, but I can't look away from his mysterious, beautiful, almost black eyes. The noise in the background has faded out to near silence. The people who were standing around us are now just a blur. The only thing I can see is the man in front of me. "Connor?" I whisper in a soft shaky voice. He removes his hands from his front pockets and in his right hand is the shiniest razor blade I have ever saw. "What are you doing?" I ask. He quickly lashes out and slices my throat.

I try to scream as I reach for my cut throat. There's so much blood. I thought Connor was dead. How can he be alive? The blood is hot and thick as it gushes from my neck onto my hands. I try to close the gaping hole in my throat, but it's useless. I scream, but nothing comes out. I need help. I need Skylar, or Chase. Where are they?

"Ava, It's me. Wake up. It's just a dream," Skylar yells.

I kick and cry. *He's here, he's right here! Why can't she see him? He has a razor! Be careful!*

"Ava, please, wake up!"

I open my eyes and it's dark. I can just make out the outline of Skylar. My face is hot from tears. I touch my face and my throat then look at my hands to make sure it's not blood. It's not. I touch my throat again and it's intact. Thank God.

"Ava, it was another dream," she says softly.

Once I realize she's right, I say, "I know. I'm sorry. I didn't mean to scare you."

"You don't have to be sorry. Are you okay?"

"He had a razor. He cut my throat." I touch my throat with both of my hands. "It seemed so real. It felt so real. I could feel the blood. I couldn't talk."

"Oh, Ava." Skylar sits on the bed and hugs me. "I'm sorry that bastard hurt you."

I can feel my body shake. "I'm tired of crying, I'm tired of these nightmares, and I'm tired of Connor still hurting me."

"I am, too."

"Well, I know one thing for sure."

"What's that?"

"This was a dream and not a memory. If he did cut my throat, I never would have survived it."

"The nightmare was that bad, huh?"

I swallow and touch my throat. "Yeah, it was."

Skylar sleeps with me that night. I don't have any more nightmares. Early the next morning there's a knock at the door. She says walking into my room, "Special delivery for Miss Ava Emerson." Skylar bounces onto the bed holding a small red, beautifully wrapped package with an attached note.

"A late Christmas gift? But from whom?" I open the gift and inside are no-bake oatmeal cookies.

"Um, my fav." Skylar takes one and pops it in her mouth. "Who sent them?"

"Xander," I say, holding the note I just read. She chokes and I laugh. "Nichole says in the note that they're from Xander."

"I knew I liked that guy. " *She makes me smile.* "How many's in there?"

I peek inside the box. "Looks like a couple dozen."

"Just leave my half on the kitchen counter and I'll eat them later."

"Your half?"

"I'm sure he meant for me to have some." She laughs at her own joke and I have to giggle. "Go change so we can go out to breakfast."

"Okay, that sounds good."

Skylar

If I could go to hell and kill Connor, I would. I can't express how much hatred I have for that man. I love Ava and he's hurt her. Even in death, he's hurting her. According to Dante, author of *The Divine Comedy*, traitors against family are punished in the lowest of the nine circles of Hell by being frozen in ice up to their neck. A wife beater is a traitor against family. If Connor had been violent only against others who were not family members, he would have been punished in Circle Seven's river of boiling blood. I used to pray to God to help her, now I pray to Xander to find Connor and get him for hurting her. Well actually, I pray to God and talk to Xander, hoping he can hear me.

She sees Doctor Adams and she also sees a counselor for her nightmares, but nothing is working. Why are her dreams suddenly changing from memories to nightmares?

Ava's been sad since Xander's death. I don't think she loved him, but I know she cared for him. When everyone went home after Christmas, she let me read what he signed to her in his new book. It was enough to make me cry, and I never cry. I called Drew and told him that I needed some time. I like him, but I'm worried that every time Ava sees him, she'll think of Xander. She doesn't need a sitter, but I have this need to protect her. Especially since I couldn't keep her safe when she married that bastard Connor.

Chase has been calling and texting Ava a lot since Xander's death. He has feelings for her, and I wish he would just confess them to her. He won't. "The time is not right," he says. I have no idea what time it needs to be, but he needs to hurry up. I told him when we were in college she was interested in him, but he didn't believe me. Then Connor came in and swooped her off her feet. *God, I hate him. I wonder what the penalty is for digging up a corpse and beating it with a baseball bat.* Whatever the punishment is, it might just be worth it. Tonight after we watched Sleepless in Seattle, I went to bed and called Chase. I want him to know that Ava's nightmares are back. There isn't anything he can do about them, but he would want to know. When I get up to get something to drink, Ava's bedroom door is ajar. When we were in college, she couldn't sleep unless the room was pitch black and quiet, but now I see a night light on and her door slightly opened. Connor has surely done a number on her. I make a mental note to buy a shovel and a baseball bat tomorrow from the department store. Peeking in her room, I ask, "Can I sleep in here?" I walk in without waiting for an answer and climb onto her large queen-sized bed.

"Can't sleep?" she asks.

"No, not really."

She's lying in bed, holding her cell phone.

"What are you doing?"

"Texting Chase."

"It seems no one can sleep tonight. What's he doing?"

"He wants to come up tomorrow for New Year's Eve."

"Let him. We don't have any plans."

"Exactly. I don't want him sitting around with us playing cards when he could be out partying it up."

I laugh. "Are we talking about the same Chase?"

She rolls her eyes. "You know we are."

"Then you should know that Chase doesn't party." I look at her and remember her amnesia. "Oh sorry, I keep forgetting."

"It's okay."

"Tell him to come, and I'll call Drew and see if he wants to come, too."

"I thought you needed some time from him?"

"I miss him. I'm ready to see him again."

"Okay, sounds good. I'll text him."

"Okay, I better call Drew to make sure he hasn't moved on without me yet."

"You don't think he has, do you?"

"Nah, it just been a few days."

The next day, the cleaners come to get the rooms ready for the guests, while Ava and I clean the house. We had family and friends here, and although everyone did their part to help with the cleanup, it still feels dirty.

We have a food delivery coming in today for the inn, so we decide to make do with that food instead of running out and fighting the crowds in the grocery store to buy more. Ava and I shower and dress in jeans and a hoodie. Chase shows up first. He brings flowers, champagne, and some store-bought hot appetizers.

"A man after my own heart," I tease. He hands me the flowers. "Not those. These." I pick up the box of Publix chicken wings and take one. "I love these."

"Good. Here, Ava, these are really for you."

"Thanks. I'll put them in water."

Ava and I put the food and the chips in our own serving dishes, and set them out on the table. I do this partly because one, it looks better, and two, I plan on taking the credit for everything when Drew gets here.

"Should I start a fire outside?" Chase asks.

"Do we have stuff for s'mores?" I ask.

Ava says, "Yeah, there's some left from the last time we had them."

"Then yes, you should definitely start a fire."

Ava stands and says, "I'll help you."

I watch as Ava and Chase walk outside carrying some old newspapers with them. I look from the large window at the interaction between them and wonder if she can see the way he looks at her. I notice she's different when he's around. She's happier. He's happier. Anyone can see the chemistry between them, except for her.

"Wake up and see it, Ava," I wanna yell.

When I hear a car pull in, I get butterflies. Drew is getting out of his car with a duffle bag, a small box, and a dozen of the most beautiful red roses I've ever seen.

"Hey," I say, walking off the steps to meet him.

He turns to look at me as a smile spreads across his beautiful face. "I've missed you," he admits right away.

That's one of the things that I like about Drew. He doesn't leave me guessing about what he's thinking. He tells me.

"It's been only a few days," I say, getting closer to him. He doesn't take his eyes off of mine.

"That may be, but it felt like much longer." He drops the flowers, box, and duffle bag onto the ground and kisses me. The kiss is deep and passionate. Things heat up quickly and I'm ready to take this to my bedroom. I've never been in a relationship where there was so much sexual attraction. It's not just sexual attraction; it's physical, emotional, intellectual, practical, and even spiritual. It's everything all combined into one. I was afraid up until this very second that it was just sexual attraction.

"How long are you staying?"

"As long as you'll have me."

"Good. You didn't bring many clothes."

"I can buy more or just keep washing these ones."

We laugh.

"Come on. Let's get you unpacked. Chase is starting a fire."

"Are we having s'mores?"

And this is why I love him. Like him. I like him. I don't love him. This is why I like him. Not love. "You know it."

While he unpacks, I put the flowers in water and carry them into the bedroom. "These smell wonderful."

"They look nice, too. I was really surprised at how big the blooms were."

"You noticed the size of the flowers' blooms?"

"Yeah, Dad made sure Xander and I knew how to buy flowers at an early age. We always bought Mom flowers for every holiday beginning when we were old enough to use the potty, I think."

"That's pretty young."

"No age is too young to make a woman feel special."

"I guess not."

"What's in the box?"

"No-bake cookies for Ava."

"From Xander?"

"Yeah, how'd you know?"

I laugh. "Nichole sent her some the other day and said they were also from Xander."

"She said that he told her to make sure she got some for every holiday."

I have to know. "Do you think he knew he was going to die?"

"I do. He dedicated his last book to her. He wrote the last book about her. He signed the proof copy for her so she'd have his complete set of books." His eyes got watery. "I think he wanted to live, but he knew he would die."

"Did he love her?"

"That, I don't know. He never said. I know that she made him happier than I've ever seen him."

Must have been love. "She was pretty happy, too."

Ava

Chase builds a fire and we talk nonstop about everything and nothing. He talks about work, and about his condo. He says the lease is coming due and he has no idea whether to renew it, or find himself someplace more permanent to live. "You're thinking of buying a house in Lake City?"

"That's where I live and work. Only makes sense to buy a house there."

"Smart ass. I mean, are you staying in Lake City forever?"

"Smart ass, huh?" He laughs. "Forever's a long time. I have no idea what the future holds, but I would like to get some place that I can make mine."

"Still have no desire to open a practice here in Savannah?"

He searches my eyes. "I'd love nothing more than to be closer to you and Skylar, but I'm not sure how it would work out. My clients are all in Lake City."

"Hey, where's the wine and the s'mores?"

I look up and Drew and Skylar are walking outside. She looks happier today than she has in the last few days since he left. "I'll get them," I say, standing to walk into the house. I turn around and ask Chase, "Do you want a beer?"

"Sure, sounds good."

I get everything together and place it all on the wooden trays. There's enough food to make two trips outside, and to feed more than the four of us.

Chase sees me through the window and comes in to help me. "You have everything?"

"I hope so. If not, I think this is plenty."

"After you."

We eat outside and Drew and Chase keep the fire going. As it gets later, the night air gets colder. I go into the house and get a couple throw blankets for everyone. The guys don't need them, but Skylar and I are freezing. We hear fireworks in the far distance, alerting us that midnight is fast approaching.

Drew talks about his military days and the explosion that killed his comrades and altered his life forever. He says, "It started off as a normal day. My comrades and I were moving things into a new location. As we got further down the dusty road, there was an Iraqi sitting on the embankment. Just him and his old dog. He nodded as we approached. Nothing seemed threatening about him or his pooch. That was our first mistake. The second mistake was to pass him. That's when the Humvee blew up. I didn't lose consciousness like my friends. I watched the man get up and walk away with his dog following behind him."

Chase listens, never interrupting. "I'm sorry for your injuries, Drew. I can't imagine what that was like for you."

"My leg was in pretty bad shape. After weeks of trying to save it to no avail, I was relieved when they said they were going to have to amputate. It was painful to try to save the mangled limb. I knew then and I know now, I'm better off without it."

Chase swallows hard and says, "Thank you for your service. It's greatly appreciated." He stands and shakes Drew's hand.

Just before midnight Drew and Skylar stand and grab the trays of food. "We're turning in. Happy New Year, and we'll see you both in the morning."

"Not waiting for midnight?"

"Not this year. I'm beat." Skylar smiles and I barely catch it. I stand and hug them both. Good night and Happy New Year."

Chase hugs Skylar and shakes Drew's hand. "You guys have to get up early for breakfast, right?"

"Not tomorrow, the guests we have didn't want breakfast. They said they'll be too hung over to eat."

"Nice," Drew says.

"I know, right?" Skylar laughs. "We did say we'd have coffee, drinks, and pastries out for them if they changed their minds."

Chase says, "Might want to have some bottled water and some packets of Tylenol on their nightstands for them when they get home tonight."

My eyes get big. "That is a brilliant idea. I'll be right back."

"Hey, wait. I was just kidding."

I yell over my shoulder. "I know, but you're a genius. I'll be right back."

As I'm collecting six bottles of water and six packets of Tylenol, I see Chase cleaning up outside. I run upstairs and place the waters and the Tylenol on the bedside tables of the guests who are staying with us. This is such a great touch, and I wish I had thought of it first. I hurry downstairs to turn the television on to watch the ball drop. Chase is standing in the kitchen putting the drinks away.

"Come on, or you'll miss it."

"Ten. Nine. Eight. Seven. Six. Five. Four, Three. Two. One," we say in unison. The ball drops and the people of New York and in the Eastern Time zone kiss. I look up at Chase and stand on my tiptoes. "Happy New Year, Chase."

"Happy New Year, Ava." He bends down and kisses me. After a quick kiss, he kisses me again just as quickly. "Here's to a bigger and better year ever."

We clink our champagne glasses and drink. "Here's to hoping."

On Saturday Chase and Drew are still here. We spent yesterday celebrating the New Year eating pork and kraut. I'm not superstitious, but I was raised eating some kind of a dinner meal with pork and cabbage every year for New Year so I have no need to change that tradition now. It's an old German tradition. They believed that eating pork and kraut on the first day of the new year would bring blessings and wealth. Who am I to argue with the Germans?

There's a knock at the door and Chase leaves to answers it.

"Babe, you're quite the cook," Drew says.

"Thanks, Babe," Skylar replies with a kiss.

I laugh. "Did anyone ever tell you guys you shouldn't have the same pet name for each other?"

Skylar licks the batter spoon. "Why?"

"Because it's like dating someone with the same name. The phone rings and the caller wants to talk to Erin. How will the person who answers the phone know whom the caller wants to talk to? The husband Aaron, or the wife Erin? It's very confusing."

Skylar looks up at Drew and says, "She's right. Babe, you'll need to come up with another pet name for me."

"Babe, ain't gonna happen. The name 'Babe' has already stuck." He kisses her again. "Sorry, Ava. 'Babe' is stayin'."

Laughing, I walk out of the room. "Just don't name your twins Erin and Aaron."

"We won't 'cause our twins will be of the same sex." I can hear Skylar laughing all the way to the foyer.

Chase is walking in from checking the mail. "Who was at the door?"

"Special delivery for Ava Emerson."

"From whom?" I take the box from Chase.

"I don't know, there's no return address on it."

We walk into the house and stop at the table in the foyer. He lays the mail down, and I open the box wrapped in brown paper. "It's postmarked Lake City, Florida."

"Maybe it's no-bake cookies," he teases.

"We could only hope." Inside the box is a pregnancy test. It's used, and it's positive. I don't touch it but show the box to Chase. He peeks inside, careful to not touch the urine-dipped stick. "I didn't see a note or a card from anyone."

"Could it be from a friend of yours?"

"I don't have any friends." My mind races with what this could mean and why would I be receiving this.

He asks, "What about your mother?"

I want to laugh. "Menopause. Maybe this is your girlfriend's?"

He holds up both hands feigning innocence. "What girlfriend?" He laughs.

"Yeah, that's what they all say. Let's ask Skylar, maybe she'll know."

We walk into the kitchen and Skylar and Drew are making out over the cake batter. I laugh. "Jesus, get a room, would ya?"

Drew stops kissing her, sweeps her off the counter, and starts to walk into the bedroom. "Great idea." She laughs and I know it's a joke.

"Not so fast, do you know what this is?"

Drew sets her down and she walks over to where we are. I shouldn't be surprised when she picks up the pregnancy test strip. She looks at me and then at Chase and says, "Congratulations, you'll both make wonderful parents."

Chase coughs, spits, and sputters, and I can only laugh and say, "It's not ours."

"Yeah, that's what they all say."

She can be so funny.

Drew walks over to join us.

"It came in the mail from Lake City. No note or card, just a positive pregnancy test."

She drops the pregnancy test strip in the box and washes her hands in the sink. "Gross. Who would and why would someone send you this nasty little thing?"

"I don't know." I walk to the trash can and throw it away before washing my hands. "I thought maybe it was a friend of yours."

"Nope, all my friends are in this house."

"Maybe it was supposed to be a pregnancy announcement, but the parents got overly excited and forgot to attach the written announcement to the fake pregnancy test strip thingy," Drew says.

"That's a good possibility. I doubt someone would actually send you an actual pregnancy test strip."

"I'm sure you're right. You guys wanna wash your hands?" I ask.

"Yeah, totally," Drew says, turning the water on high.

Later that night, I fall asleep on the couch and Chase wakes me up to go to bed. I stagger into the bedroom and climb under the heavy blankets. He tucks me in before turning off the lamp on the nightstand. Bending down, he kisses me on my forehead.

Chase

When I kiss Ava goodnight, I say, "Sweet dreams, Ava."

She mumbles something that I can hardly hear. "Connor's coming."

It sounded like she said, "Connor's coming." *He's dead.* What is she talking about? I stand over her bed and watch her. The muted light from the other room gives off just enough glow that I can see she's sleeping. I kiss her again. "Good night, Ava."

She whispers, "He's mad."

My eye twitches at her words. Instead of sleeping upstairs in the bed and breakfast, I get a pillow and blanket from her bedroom closet and make a bed on her floor. If she thinks Connor's coming for her, I plan to be here to intercept him. Every time I think about what Connor may have done to her, guilt creeps into my soul and takes over every emotion I have. I have so much guilt over not protecting Ava while she was married. I didn't know what was happening to her, but I should have been a better friend. I should have insisted on seeing her weekly. I should have insisted on talking to her. If I had, I would have known something was wrong. Connor always made it sound like he was doing great and wonderful things with her. He always made it sound like she was happy and they had this great and terrific life. The guilt still creeps into my soul and reminds me I was not a friend. I suspected something was wrong, and yet I turned a blind eye. I will never forgive myself for what I let him do to her. I want her to get her memory back, but in a way, I don't. I think her amnesia is protecting her from her real-life nightmares. If her dreams are anything like the nightmare she lived, I'm not sure she can survive them again, even in a memory.

When she moans in her sleep, I rush over to her. That bastard doesn't stand a chance of getting close to her tonight. Not with me here with her. "I'm here, Ava." I touch her dark hair. "It's just me."

When she calms I know that her dream is a thing of the past. I return to my makeshift bed and stare at the white ceiling. My mind plays over my relationship with Connor. If I had told Ava my true feelings for her before Connor met her, maybe all of this could have been avoided. Maybe she would have been with me and not him. I want to tell her now, but it's so soon after Xander's death. It's not the right time. It's never the right time with Ava. I want it to be perfect. When I finally tell her how I feel, I want everything to be perfect. I want her mind to be on me, not on the passing of Xander. Or the abuse she's suffered. Or the... I could come up with a million reasons why the timing isn't right. I need to tell her. She needs to know. If she reciprocates my feelings, then I'll plan an engagement, if not… it could ruin our friendship. Is it worth that? Could I live everyday and not be friends with her or have a strained friendship with her? I listen to the faint sound of Ava sleeping peacefully and the answer is no, I can't. If this is all I get for the rest of my life, then I'll take it over a strained relationship any day.

When the sun comes up, I stow my bedding in the closet, and I return to my own room.

Skylar

"I think you should tell her how you feel. She should know. She has a right to know." I stand there with my hands on my hips, trying to talk some sense into the ever-so-smart attorney. I've never met a stupider man in my entire life. Well, that might be a lie. But he's an attorney, so he should be smarter than that.

"Skylar, I'm not going to tell her."

"Tell her what?" Ava walks into the room.

"Chase has something to tell you." *There I said it.* "He's been keeping a secret from you for a while now." *I feel better already. It may not have been the smartest thing to say, but it needed to be said.*

She looks serious. "Oh, what is it?"

He glares at me before looking at Ava. His look softens. *Of course it does.* He takes a deep breath. My heart beats faster now with excitement. Because now, he's going to tell her he loves her, she's going to say it back and they'll live happily-ever-after with lots and lots of cute little babies. "I don't know how to say this."

Chase clasps his hands together. I squeeze Drew's hand too tightly and he moans. "Oh, sorry." I loosen my hold slightly as I watch this historic moment.

Ava looks at him nervously "Just say it. Whatever it is, I can take it."

He swallows hard. I lean forward almost falling over. He says, "Your tires on your car all need replaced. I was outside and noticed they're in pretty bad shape."

I wanna beat my head against the door. I opened the door for you. I gave you an opportunity and you blow it on some bad tires. I can't take it.

"Oh, I can take care of that this week. But Skylar said you've been keeping a secret from me for a while."

"Yeah, she's right. I've known about it since before Thanksgiving. I just didn't want to tell you then. Not when you had so much going on with Xander and the holidays, and all." He looks at me before looking back at Ava. "I can take the car to the tire shop today."

"Great, thanks. I'd appreciate that."

"Chase, can I see you outside for a minute?" I don't wait for an answer. I storm past him and Ava and right out the door. He follows me, as he should. As soon as the door closes, I say, "What in the hell was that?"

"What? Her tires are bald. She should be aware of it before she gets a flat."

I growl and storm back into the house. It's useless trying to talk to him. Drew and Chase take Ava's car into town to get new tires, while we stay behind and run the afternoon tea. Lou Ann and Steve are right, things are slower in the winter months here. I thought it would have been busier in the winter. I guess people want to see the gardens and parks of Savannah in full bloom.

"Maybe next year if we can afford it, we could close down for the month of January," I suggest.

"Skylar, if you and Drew want to do something, I can stay here and run the inn. We have been pretty slow."

"No, I was thinking maybe next year, we could close down and all of us could actually go and do something together. Go skiing in Colorado, or surfing in Hawaii."

"That would be nice, but I don't have a *we* and Chase may be in a relationship by next year."

I highly doubt that. "Well, if we're all still single or dating each other, maybe we could think about it for next January."

"Sound like a very unlikely plan. But okay, it sounds good to me."

On Sunday, Chase leaves to go home and Drew works from his computer. Ava and I prepare food and bake for the meals served at the inn. I once thought I would dread doing this every Sunday, but I actually look forward to it. We always try new recipes and for the day, we eat whatever we make. So, it's breakfast all day long. Ava seems happier and I give Chase the credit for that. He's so stubborn. I wish he would just finally tell her how he feels.

I walk into the bedroom where Drew is working on his computer. "What are you working on?"

He smiles and it lights up his entire face. "I have this idea of how I can honor my brother's legacy."

"Xander's or Jami's?"

"I'm not sure yet. But look at what I've come up with." He angles his computer around for me to see. "It's not done yet and it's still just a rough draft, but I hope you can see my vision through the mess."

I study the draft that's pulled up on his computer. "Babe, that's incredible."

"Really?"

"Yeah. I think this is more Xander than Jami, but yeah, I can totally see this being a hit."

"Do you have a location?"

"Tybee Island."

"Perfect. It's my favorite place. Let me know if I can help you do anything."

"I will. Thanks, babe."

Later that night, Ava has another dream. She wakes up crying and in a cold sweat. She refuses to tell me what this dream is about, and she gets out of bed and showers at 3:00 am. I wanna help her, but how? What did that bastard do to her? Deciding I won't be able to sleep, I make some coffee and also shower.

Just before the noon tea, a man comes into the inn looking for Ava. He's dressed in jeans and a blue jean button-up shirt. He's older, tall, and extremely good looking, with silvering just at his temples. He waits in the foyer while I get Ava from the back.

"Hi, I'm Ava." She greets him warmly. She's always so sweet and happy with everyone. No one who doesn't know her would know about the demons that haunt her. "This is my friend, Skylar."

He reaches his hand out for hers. "Hi, I'm Luke Tanner. I'm the recipient of this dinner card you sent me." He pulls out an Olive Garden gift card from his front pocket. *I'm clueless. Is Ava randomly sending good-looking men dinner gift cards? Mmm, that might be a great idea. They come to thank her and bam, she has a dinner date! What a genius idea!*

"Oh. My. God." Ava looks excited. "The girl you helped with the children, they were here a few weeks ago."

"Olivia. Yes, we met. She said they're moving back home to Texas."

Ava asks, "Do you want to stay for tea?"

He pokes his head into the tearoom. "No, thanks. I can't stay. I just wanted to return the gift card back to you, and to thank you for the sweet card you sent me."

"You're welcome, but why are you giving me back the gift card?" He hands it to her, but she doesn't take it. "I bought it for you as a thank you for helping them."

"I know and I appreciate that."

"So why are you trying to give it back?"

He laughs. "It's kind of embarrassing." *Then please tell, I think to myself. He's gay and he's still in the closet? No, that's not it. People don't care about that anymore. One thing this generation has learned to do is to accept other people. Love is love, no matter the gender. This generation has learned to love one another. We've made progress! Just compare now with, say, fifty or a hundred years ago. Or maybe he's married and he was here visiting his girlfriend? That could be it. People will always frown on cheaters.* "I'm single and I don't like eating out alone," he admits. *Wow, I didn't see that coming. Hi, I'm Skylar. I'll be more than happy to have dinner with you. Drew! I'm seeing Drew. Damnit!*

"Oh," Ava says, surprised. "Then you should save it for when you're seeing someone."

"That may be awhile. I'm not looking for anyone and I think this has an expiration date on it." He turns it over too quickly to read what's written in fine print. "Here, you should use it. It was very sweet of you to send it to me, and I do appreciate it."

Ava starts to take it from him when I get an idea. "We know a friend who's moving into the area."

Ava retracts her hand. "We do?"

"Yes, her name's Nichole and she's single." *Sort of. Well she will be.* "She just bought the old bakery over on Magnolia Street."

"A blind date?" He laughs. "No, thank you. Been on too many of those and they've never worked out."

I take a step forward. "But you haven't met this one."

"Let me guess. She's stunning, and beautiful, and smart, and she's educated."

He looks at me and I stare back. "Yes, she's all those things."

"So were all of the other ones." He doesn't wait for Ava to take the card from him. He places it on the foyer table and says, "Thank you, Ava. It's very sweet, but you and your husband should enjoy a nice dinner out this evening."

"You're welcome. It was wonderful what you did for Olivia and her daughters."

"I would do it again for anyone. No one, male or female, should have to be treated like that."

Ava walks him to the door and opens it for him. "Thank you for stopping by, Luke. It was nice meeting you."

"You, too, Ava. Skylar, it was my pleasure."

"See ya."

She closes the door and looks at me. "A blind date, really. You don't even know him."

"If he's rescuing woman from assholes who beat on them, he's perfect for Nichole. I don't have to know anything else about him to see that he's a great guy."

"Well, you might be right, but I think you scared him off."

"Nah, I just piqued his interest. I'm pretty sure we'll be seeing Luke Tanner again."

That night, Ava has another nightmare. Each one is becoming worse than the last one, and they are coming more and more frequently. I tell her to call Doctor Adams. Something needs to be done. She agrees to call, but I don't believe her. When I know she'll be okay, I return to my bedroom where Drew is sitting up in bed waiting for me. "He did a real number on her, didn't he?"

"He did." I climb into bed. "I think her amnesia is protecting her, but I also think that if she remembers, there won't be anything left to haunt her."

"Is she strong enough to handle the truth? I mean, when or if she remembers her past, can she deal with the things that her husband did to her?"

"I have no idea. Can it be any worse than the dreams she's having?"

Drew thinks for a minute. "I'm afraid that it can."

Ava

I don't recall having nightmares when I slept with Xander. When Chase was here this last time, I didn't have nightmares then either. It seems like I have nightmares only when I sleep alone, which is all of the time. They're more vivid and violent than before. Connor is angrier and more aggressive in my current dreams. When I wake up from them, Skylar wants to talk about them. I always tell her I can't remember them. The sad truth is, I'll never be able to forget them. I can't talk about them. I can't say the things that happen to me in my dreams, at least not to Skylar. I don't want the images to haunt her, too.

I'm tired, but I'm too frightened to sleep, and I'm too scared to turn the lights off. I lie in bed, awake, staring at the walls. Connor and I started off having dinner in a restaurant, but we ended up in the car. He threatens to kill me, but the reason is unclear.

I should see Doctor Adams, but he suggested at my last visit giving me a sleep aid. I've researched Ambien and I don't want anything to do with that. Tylenol PM might be okay to take. I haven't slept well since Xander's death. I was hoping since the holidays were over, maybe I would get into a normal routine. You know, sleep all night without waking up, thinking a knife is being held to my throat. *Why didn't I just leave? If I couldn't leave, why didn't I just kill him? Surely I would have gotten off. There's battered woman's syndrome. That's a defense they use in court. I didn't do either. I stayed with him and I excluded my family and friends from my life, but why?* I walk out into the living room and knock on Skylar's bedroom door.

"Come in," Drew says.

They are both up watching television. "What's up?" Skylar asks, sitting up in the bed.

"Since we don't have any reservations this week, I was thinking about going to Lake City for a few days. Do you guys want to come with me?"

"You're seeing Doctor Adams?"

"It's the weekend."

"That's right."

Lake City holds the answers to my past and maybe a trip back will stir some different kinds of memories for me. "I want to see Mom, Dad, and Chase."

Skylar says, "I think someone should be here at the inn."

Maybe she's right. "Maybe I shouldn't go either."

"Drew and I can handle the inn, you take a mini vacation to Lake City."

When I first thought about going, I thought it was a good idea. Now, I'm not sure. "Drew, do you mind? It's not really fair expecting you to run the inn."

"I don't do anything when I'm here. Skylar does it all, I just keep her company."

"I'll be gone for only a couple days."

"Stay as long as you need to. Let us know when you're packed, and we'll walk you to the door."

I arrive in Lake City just after 3:00 pm. I didn't call Mom, Dad, or Chase to tell them I was coming. My first stop is the accident site. When I arrive there, the wooden cross is tattered and worn, but it's still standing. Parking the car, I get out and walk the short distance to it. Just like the last time, white calla lilies are lying on the ground. No card is attached and no other flowers are left. A small red toy truck is lying in the dirt near the cross. I look out into the open field where Skylar said the car rolled over and landed on its top. The grass is grown over and there's nothing to suggest that a fatal car accident happened.

Not much traffic is on the road this time of day, so I drive to Connor's final resting place. Not so much to pay my respects, but to see if a memory will surface... something... anything. I need to face my fears. I want to remember so I can move on. I used to be content with forgetting the past and living for today, but now I'm fearful to fall asleep. I'm afraid of what will haunt me in my dreams. I need to know what happened to me. What happened on the night that changed my life forever? The night that Connor died.

The cemetery is eerie and cold. I park my car and walk towards the black granite tombstone. I think about Nichole and the loss of her son. Even though he was a monster, he was still her son. I know she loved him. I like her and it's sad to think about everything she's gone through in her marriage. Her son's death. Her husband's abuse. *Did Connor learn to be abusive from his father? Is that why he beat me? I have to wonder if Connor hit others before me. Was Connor capable of hitting his mother? God, I feel sick to my stomach. What if Nichole was abused by her husband and her son? A tear slides down my cheek as I envision the nightmare she could have lived. Do I dare to ask her? It's none of my business.* I don't walk the rest of the way to Connor's grave. He doesn't deserve my visit. There are no answers for me here. I turn to leave without saying a prayer. Without saying a goodbye. Without shedding a tear.

When I leave I drive by Nichole and Brett's house. From the outside it looks like an upper-class home. You could almost imagine the laughter coming from inside the house. You could almost picture the wonderful holidays being shared, and the Sunday dinners being prepared inside. Looks sure are deceiving. There's a FOR SALE sign in the front yard that I'm surprised to see. It makes me wonder whether Brett isn't trying to sell the house from under Nichole. I make a mental note to mention this to Chase. I do think it's best to get rid of all bad memories from her past so she can move forward to a much brighter and happier future.

I call Chase to see if he wants to meet me for dinner. He thinks it's a joke at first, until he realizes I'm waiting for him outside of his office building. "I'm glad you're here," he says excitedly. "Come on up while I wrap things up."

His office is the same place where Connor worked prior to his death. I haven't been here since before the accident. I don't remember anyone and if they speak to me, I won't know who they are. "Okay, I'll be right there." I have issues, but I don't need to make them Chase's problems. "Meet me at the elevator."

"I will. I can't wait to see you."

No matter what, Chase always makes me feel welcome, and he always makes me feel like I'm the most important person in the room. When I step off the elevator, he's there waiting for me. We hug, and then he walks me to his office with his arm wrapped securely around me. It feels good to be here with him.

"So what brings you to Lake City?" I sit down and he sits on the other side of his desk.

What do I say to that? He's my friend. He needs to know the truth. "Searching for answers."

"To your past?"

I nod. "It's the only way I can move forward." Do I tell him about my most recent nightmare? My dreams have been memories and I don't think this one is any different. "I had another nightmare last night."

"I know, Skylar called me. What was it about?"

Of course she did. I don't want to remember, but sadly, I can't forget. "I think I was pregnant."

"What?"

"In one of my dreams, we had a horrible argument about a baby, or a pregnancy, or something to do with a child."

"It's vague?"

Closing my eyes, I say, "Some parts are, but some parts are vivid and it feels so real. His anger is so… frightening. He was furious. Madder than I have ever dreamed about him."

"I'm sorry." He leans up in his leather chair.

"It's not your fault. I think if I face my past, maybe… hopefully, I can move forward to a brighter future."

"How do you plan to get the answers you need?"

"When I sold and moved out of the house, what I didn't take with me, I put in storage."

"And you're up to this?"

I have to be. "It's time."

He smiles. "Okay. I'll be right there with you."

"You will?" I smile.

"Of course. You're my girl, I wouldn't let you do this alone. We'll start first thing in the morning." He thinks for a moment. "You weren't wanting to start tonight, were you?"

"No, tomorrow's perfect. Thank you, Chase."

He places some things in his briefcase before leaving. As we walk out of his office building, I see a woman watching me. It's Lorraine, who was Connor's legal secretary when he was alive. I also remember her from the cemetery. As we walk toward the elevator, she continues to stare at me. She doesn't smile or wave, and she doesn't seem overly friendly either. I notice her bleach-blonde hair and her perfectly shaped painted red lips. She stops walking and watches Chase and me until we round the corner to the elevator.

We have dinner at the Main Street Deli and Pub. It's nothing fancy, but it's always good food and music. Once we're done, we walk along the brick roads of downtown. The area is small and quaint. The store owners leave white Christmas lights outside of the shops all year long. It reminds me of a scene in a painting. It's peaceful and tranquil. We get coffee and drink it outside of the courthouse.

Chase puts his arm over the back of the wooden and metal bench. "I remember Mom and Dad bringing me here when I was little to play in the splash park."

"Seems odd to have a splash park outside of a courthouse."

"Not a likely place for sure. But it seems to work well for the nearby families."

Lake City is a great place to raise a family. "I wish I could remember if I came here as a child."

"After tomorrow, maybe you'll get all of your memories back. The good and the bad."

"That would be nice." *I'll need something good to balance the bad memories and emotions.*

On the way back to his office to get my car, he says, "Did your parents want to join us for dinner?"

"They don't know I'm here."

"You didn't call them?"

"I needed some time. I need time to think."

"Are you done thinking now? Because if you are, you may want to call them and tell them you're in town."

I giggle. "I think I'm done." I call Mom and it goes right to voicemail. My call to Dad also goes to voicemail. I leave them a quick message that I'm in town for a few days and to call me when they get this.

"Are you staying with me?" Chase asks. "I have a spare bedroom you can sleep in."

"Sure, sounds good. I don't want to stay at Mom and Dad's if they're not home."

I get in my car and follow Chase to his condo. He shows me around and I put my bag in the spare room. I'm surprised to see some photos of Skylar, him, and me framed and displayed in his home. "Did you frame this?" I ask, holding up a framed photo.

"No. You and Skylar gifted me those throughout the years."

Some of the photos of us are fun and silly. Others are more serious and almost intimate. He and Skylar look like a couple. They look happy and cute together. "Why didn't you and Skylar ever date?"

He almost chokes on his beer. "Because I was never interested in Skylar."

Chapter Six: More Surprises

Chase

I guess I'm hiding my feelings from Ava better than I thought. She still thinks that Skylar and I should be a couple. Little does she know it's her where my heart is, not with Skylar. "So," she says as she kicks her feet up on the glass coffee table, "you have this big fancy condo and no one to share it with?"

"I've been thinking about changing that," I say seriously.

"You have a girlfriend?"

"No, I've been thinking about getting a dog." She tosses a pillow at me. "What?"

"Chase, you're a great guy. You need to share your wonderful life with someone."

"I will one day." *Maybe.* "I'm holding out."

"For what?"

"For the perfect girl." *I've already found her, I'm just waiting for her to realize I'm here sitting in front of her.*

She thinks for a minute. "Does the perfect person even exist?"

"Yes, I'm certain of it."

Once we go to bed, I don't sleep in the bedroom; I sleep on the couch, instead. If Ava starts to dream, I want to be able to hear her before the nightmare has taken over her slumber. I wish there was a way to stop the nightmares before they begin. She doesn't deserve this. She doesn't deserve the life that Connor gave her. When I hear her moan, I don't rush in to be by her side. I don't want to frighten her more than she already is. I cough loudly enough for her to hear me, instead. As long as she wakes up from the dream, she should be good to continue on to a restful sleep. I hope.

In the morning we shower and put on old clothes before heading out to the storage unit. I stop and get some trash bags in case she decides it's time to let go of some of the stuff she's been holding onto. I don't know everything that she stored, so I'm not sure what to expect.

Just like Ava's house she shared with Connor, everything is stacked meticulously. There are boxes and furniture. I just sit with her on the concrete floor as she goes through photos, cards, papers, and receipts. I can't help her decide what to keep and what to discard. I'm just here for support in case she finds something or remembers something.

"Who's this girl with Connor?"

I lean over and remove the large stack of photos from her hand. There are several dozen pictures of Connor and his secretary, Lorraine. The picture on top of the stack was taken at a holiday party. I remember it well. Ava wasn't at this party, Connor said she was home ill. Connor and Lorraine hung around each other a lot, and I never understood their working/nonworking relationship.

"It's Lorraine, Connor's legal secretary."

She takes the photo and looks at it again. "That's Lorraine?"

"Yeah. You remember her, right?"

"Lorraine's a blonde, right? She was at your office yesterday."

"That's right. She goes from blonde to brunette depending on the time of the month."

She laughs, although it wasn't meant to be a joke. "She looks different in this photo."

"That's definitely Lorraine. I see her everyday and she looks different to me every time I see her." *I think to myself that Lorraine's one odd girl, but I don't say that.* I watch as Ava looks carefully at each photo before tossing them in the trash.

She keeps all of the photos of Connor alone and tosses out all of the couples pictures or group pictures with the two of them.

She says, "I think Nichole would like to have these."

I look inside the box at the photos of just Connor. "I think these will mean a lot to her."

"Me, too." She pauses and says, "Hey, I forgot to tell you that I drove by their family home last night and it's up for sale."

"I know. I'm hoping it sells quickly."

"Brett agreed to the sale."

"It was his idea. He claims to want out of this marriage as much as Nichole."

"What's he up to?"

"I have no idea. But selling their combined assets and banking the money will make the divorce easier for both of them. The only thing they'll need to do is divide the money, IRA's, and things like that."

"What about the bakery she just bought?"

"That came out of her own money. She had an inheritance from her grandparents and she invested it. Nichole kept the money from him and invested wisely, the money grew, and she kept reinvesting it."

Good for her. I wish everyone could be so fortunate to have a chance to start over so easily.

"What is it you're looking for exactly?"

"Proof that I was pregnant once, or maybe some brochures on adoption. My recent nightmares are about a child and I need to know if it was my pregnancy that sent Connor into a rage."

"I can't imagine that you would have let yourself get pregnant in the conditions you were living in."

"I know, me either. It doesn't make any sense."

"Maybe your dreams this time aren't a memory."

She reaches for another box. "Maybe, but I doubt it."

I suppose it was wishful thinking. "Here, I'll look through the receipts while you look through the other stuff."

Out of everything in the storage room, Ava ended up keeping only a small box of photos and some legal documents. She stands and dusts off her clothes. "Well, my past isn't in this room."

"That's a good thing." We lock up the storage unit, make several trips to the dumpster, then head to my condo. "What are you going to do with the rest of the furniture in the unit?"

"Keep it in case I need it or someone I know needs it. Some of the furniture belongs to Skylar."

"Did your Mom and Dad call you back yet?"

"Nope, not yet."

"You want to have dinner in Gainesville with me tonight? We can eat at the Macaroni Grill."

"I love that place."

"Good, me, too." We shower and get ready for dinner. We both dress in jeans and she wears a black sweater. I decide on a black button-up shirt to match her attire. After dinner we walk through the mall. We don't shop for anything special, we just window shop. There's a new store called Dream Time that I want to walk in. The store says it specializes in restful sleep. It has pillows, feathered mattress covers, scented candles, night lights, expensive bedding, soft music, and waterfalls. We walk around the room and there are even dream catchers on the makeshift windows.

"Is there something I can help you with?" a saleswoman asks.

Ava says, "We're just looking, thank you."

I look around the room and say, "I understand about the bedding and pillows providing a better night's sleep, but how can the waterfalls and the music help?"

"Follow me."

We follow her to where the different-sized waterfalls are located in the room. The different sizes of waterfalls range from some that will fit on your nightstand to some that stand nearly 12 foot high. We listen to the soft trickle of water briefly before the saleswoman says, "It's peaceful, right?"

Ava yawns. "A little bit."

The woman laughs. "We get that response all of the time. The soothing sound helps to put you into a deeper slumber and keep you there."

"And the music?" I ask.

"It serves the same purpose."

"You wouldn't need both of them."

She says, "That all depends. Have you ever been to a waterfall? Maybe Ichetucknee Springs?"

"Sure."

"Did you hear the birds chirping in the background?" She pauses and gives us time to think about it "Maybe during a picnic?" When I understand, she says, "See, it's all wrapped up together to create a more relaxing, deeper rest."

I think I like this idea. Ava looks like she's ready to leave. "So, if you get the chirping birds, you don't really need the large waterfall, right? The smaller one will work just as good?"

"Correct."

Okay, I like this store. "I saw some candles when we came in."

"Right this way." Ava and I follow her to the candle display.

"Chase, you really need all this to help you sleep?" Ava asks.

It's not for me, it's her I'm shopping for. "Work can be very stressful," I lie. *Well, it's not a total lie. Work can be very stressful.*

To my surprise, they make and sell scented flameless candles. I purchase the two sets of the vanilla-scented, battery-operated three-piece candles, batteries for the candles, two CD's with chirping birds, and two smaller-size waterfalls.

"I think you're trying to set the mood for a special someone." Ava teases as we walk out to the car. *If only she knew she is my special someone.*

We stop and have a drink at Phish Heads before heading to the condo. I didn't expect to see Ava this weekend, but I couldn't be happier to have her here. When we get home, I take my purchases out of the trunk and carry them into the condo. Ava helps me set everything out, keeping one set of everything in the bag. She puts the batteries in the candles before she starts to carry them into my bedroom.

"It's not for me," I say, walking into the guest room that she slept in.

I fill the waterfall with distilled water and turn it on. Ava turns the switches on for the candles and they glow and flicker like real wax candles. The birds chirp from the CD player and she laughs. "I feel like I should be on a tropical island."

"Well, you're in Florida. Does that count?"

"Lake City, Florida? No, not hardly."

She lies on the bed and closes her eyes. "This is pretty relaxing."

"Good, let me know if it stops your nightmares." I walk out of the room and place the bag with the extra items near the front door.

"Chase?" she says from the other room.

"Yeah?"

She walks out into the living room. "You got this stuff for me?"

"Maybe with luck, they'll slow down your nightmares."

She walks over to me and kisses me. "Thank you."

I hug her and hold her. "I just hope it helps." *Is this a good time to tell her how I feel? She kissed me. It feels right. She smells of vanilla and cranberries. Maybe I should buy some vanilla- and cranberry-scented candles. I'd sleep like I lived on cloud 9 if I did.*

Ava

Chase surprises me at every turn. He's thoughtful, giving, caring, and good looking. I never expected to stay with him this weekend. I showed up unexpected, thinking I would have dinner with him and maybe see him one other time before leaving, but I've spent the entire weekend with him, never leaving his side.

He's single and it's the weekend. I would have expected him to have plans with some guys or a girl. *He doesn't date? Why? Is he that picky and no one is good enough for him? No, that's not it. Is he that busy with work that there's no time for a relationship? I didn't see him open his briefcase once this weekend.*

We go to bed and I turn off two of the flameless candles and leave one on. It's just enough lighting. The birds chirp softly and the waterfall contributes to a calming ambience. Closing my eyes I drift off into a peaceful sleep. I don't dream of angry men, or abuse, or fights. I don't dream of injuries, deaths, or trauma. Instead, I dream of sandy beaches, piña coladas, and cabana boys.

I wake up feeling more rested than I ever have. I shower and make coffee while Chase sleeps on the couch. He wakes up and stretches his neck.

"Good morning." He smiles.

"Good morning. Stiff neck?" I ask.

He moves his head in a circular motion. "No, it's good. How did you sleep?"

"Great. That stuff really works."

"Good, glad to hear it."

I look in the fridge and see some turkey bacon and egg whites. "Breakfast?"

"Sounds good. Let me shower then I'll help."

I hand him his coffee and say, "I got this, take your time in the shower."

He folds his blanket and takes his things to the bedroom while I start cooking. It seems so natural to be in his home making breakfast. I wonder have I ever done this before? Cooking for just Chase and me?

During breakfast Mom and Dad call to tell me they went to the Florida Keys for the weekend. When I first arrived, I actually planned to stay longer than just the weekend. But after a good night's sleep, I plan to return to the inn later today.

"How long are you staying?" Chase asks.

"I'm heading back to the inn after breakfast."

"I hate to see you go."

"Yeah, me, too, but I can't leave Skylar and Drew there to run it alone."

"Speaking of Skylar and Drew, how are those two?"

"In love, I think."

"I kind of thought that when I was there last. I'm amazed at how well they get along."

"Me, too. They're a good match, though."

"Does it bother you seeing him everyday?"

"What do you mean?"

"Since he looks so much like Xander? I wondered how you felt about that."

"Drew and Xander are so different, and because of that I don't think I notice the similarities in their looks anymore."

"That's good. I was afraid it would be hard on you."

"It's not. No need to worry about that. He's great with Skylar. I'm thrilled for the both of them."

"Me, too. She deserves to be happy."

"She does."

We clean up after breakfast and I leave to go home, taking the extra items that Chase bought from Dream Time. I drive through Savannah and to the bakery that Nichole has purchased. It's even cuter than I remembered. She'll be able to do great things with this place. A little bit of paint and some power washing, and this place will be ready for business. Magnolia Street. What a cute street name. "The Sweet Shop on Magnolia Street." What a cute name for a bakery. "Mocha, Muffins, and Macaroons." What fun way to name a bakery. "Mocha, Macaroons, and Muffin Tops." Uh, maybe not that name. I laugh to myself. It's not my business to name. After feeling better from a weekend away, I head home to the inn.

Drew and Skylar are playing poker and having pizza for dinner. I notice that Skylar is wearing a tank top, underwear, and socks. Drew is wearing gym shorts and no top. His prosthetic leg is attached above his knee. The house is clean and the inn is empty. I try to not let the empty rooms bother me. I know we'll have some down time, and this is one of those times.

As I carry in the things that Chase bought me to my room, Skylar asks, "Did you do some shopping?"

"A little." I don't tell her about the items Chase bought to help me sleep. "We went to the Gainesville mall."

"Dinner at the Macaroni Grill?" she calls from the other room.

"I've never had a bad meal there." I walk out of my room and sit on the couch.

"Me, either. How's your mom and dad?"

"Vacationing in the Keys."

"No way."

"Yep, I didn't even see them while I was there."

"That's too bad. Did you get some things done?"

"I cleaned out some junk from the storage unit, and I spent some time with Chase." *I also said goodbye to Connor. I don't say that. She doesn't need to know I went to the cemetery and it was my last visit there.*

"You're feeling better?"

I smile. "I am."

Skylar draws another card from the stack.

"Good. Nichole rented a room and she's staying upstairs. She closes on her property this week and she wants some help getting it ready."

"Wait. She's here now? I didn't see her car."

"No, she's gone out to get some stuff. She'll be back later." I'm just about to say something when she yells, "I WIN, BITCHES!"

Drew sits up and looks to make sure she's not cheating. I laugh at the tone she uses.

"Take it off, babe." She laughs. She sits back and watches as he stands.

"Wait, you guys are playing strip poker?"

"Yep, sure are, and Drew's the loser."

They both laugh and I have never seen her so happy.

"Hello, I'm in the room, remember."

"It's okay, Ava. I came prepared for this." He removes his gym shorts only to reveal another pair beneath the pair he just removed.

Everyone laughs and Skylar says, "You suck."

"And you cheat."

She tosses a pillow at him and laughs louder. "I do, it's true."

The bell over the door chimes and I walk out to meet our guest. Nichole is walking into the inn. "Hey, closing on the bakery this week, are you?"

"I am. Isn't it exciting?" She hugs me before I can answer her. "How are you?"

"I'm good. I went to Lake City for a couple days."

"Skylar told me. Is everything okay?"

"I have these recurrent nightmares."

"Of the abuse?"

"Yeah, but because of my amnesia, I can't make any sense of them." She looks so sad when she looks at me. "He's always so mad and mean and I never know why."

"I'm sorry, Ava."

"Anyway." I hurry to change the subject. "I went the storage unit and I have a box of photos of Connor I thought you'd like to have."

"Thank you. He was my son and I loved him. But I never approved of his behavior. Ever."

I want to ask her did he treat her the same way he treated me, but I can't. I can't ask her that. I don't want her to have the same nightmares I have. I was in a great mood up until this point. I need to change the subject. "So, I just drove by the bakery. It looks great with the 'Sold' sign out front of it."

"I close on Wednesday. I'm so nervous and excited at the same time."

"I'm thrilled for you."

"Thank you. I went out and bought some cleaning supplies, cookbooks, and some things I thought I would need."

"I saw your house for sale in Lake City."

"Selling it fully furnished, too. I didn't want anything from there."

"I put in storage some things that I may never use from my house. You're more than welcome to everything and anything in there if you want them."

"Thank you, Ava. That's really nice, but I think you should donate them to a women's battered shelter. Give it to someone like us, someone who could use it to better their lives."

My skin prickles on my arm. *Women like us. There's more of us. It's like we're labeled, which we are. We all have this black cloud that hangs over us.* "I have no idea why I didn't think about doing that. I'll call around this week to find a place that'll come and pick it up."

"We'd all sleep better at night if everyone were as kind and giving as you are."

I wish it were that easy. Then I think about Luke Tanner rescuing Olivia and her twins. One good deed at a time. I need to change the subject. "Well, as you can see we're having our slow time, so whatever you need, let us know and we'll all pitch in and make it happen."

"Thank you. I will."

Later that night, I go to bed and read. I pull out a notebook that Xander had while he was staying here. Flipping through the pages, I stop when I see his handwriting. It reads:

Xander's Funny Bucket List Of Things To Do With Ava

I get choked up thinking he made a bucket list, and I have no idea what could be funny about it. Drying my tears, I force myself to look at his list.

1- Drink blue Gatorade from a Windex bottle during the afternoon tea at the inn.

2- Go to McDonald's and order a happy meal, ask if it's happy hour, then order a McBeer.

3- Go to PetSmart and buy bird seed and ask the cashier how long it takes for the birds to grow.

4- Walk into Sea World with a fishing pole.

5- Go to a library and ask for a book on how to read.

6- Stick an ice cream cone on my forehead and tell a child I'm a unicorn.

7- Sit in a car with Ava's hair dryer and point it at oncoming cars. See how many cars slow down.

8- Post a Post It note on Ava's guest doors saying, "I know where you are."

9- Eat vanilla pudding from a mayonnaise jar.

10: Go to an ATM, make a withdrawal, and yell, "I won, I won."

I laugh so hard I cry. I scan the book looking for other notes or letters he may have written. Sadly, this is the only one. I reread it, laughing just as hard as I did the first time I read it.

That night I dream of Xander and his funny bucket list. I'm happy when Xander visits me in my dream. We laugh and he's sweet. He's white and bright, almost angelic. He's exactly what I would expect him to be. Xander tells me that on Earth a happy life is waiting for me and that I have an admirer and he's exactly what I deserve. I don't believe him, but I sleep better knowing that Xander is in a good place. I pray for more visits from him.

The next day, Rachael drives down and we all go furniture shopping with Nichole for the bakery and the upstairs apartment. Nichole also finds a great sale on bistro tables for the bakery, and a sale on magnolia floral material. She's planning on making valances and matching tablecloths for the bakery. I didn't know she could sew, and I'm looking forward to seeing the finished product.

On Wednesday, Nichole is beyond excited for the next chapter of her life. Chase is coming up to go with her while she closes on her new business. I'm excited and it's fun to watch her. She even bought a new dress and shoes for today. Skylar and Drew also bought champagne for a celebratory toast for later.

As soon as they close on the building, Chase said he'll take her over to get the permits she needs to open the bakery. The bakery won't be ready to open for a couple months, but he wants to make sure she has everything in order.

I don't think I've ever seen someone so excited. When Skylar and I bought the inn, I was more frightened than anything. We moved to a new state where we didn't know anyone. I was more frightened for her than for myself. She gave up her job to follow my dream. I look at Skylar and she looks so happy. Her life is in a good place. I'm glad that this move has worked out for her. She deserves to be happy.

Chase and I talk or text every night, every morning, and sometimes throughout the day. He's funny and smart and it's a great combination. He tells me he's been sleeping in his guest room at his condo and the ambience of the room has been making him sleep through his alarm. I know he's teasing and it makes me laugh. I'm actually sleeping better at night, so he can make fun all he wants. He's a great guy and I love that we're friends. I just wish he could find someone to share his life.

"I guess we're meeting everyone over at the bakery. Chase said he'll call when they're done with the paperwork," I say, slipping on a sweatshirt.

"I'm excited for her." Skylar looks at Drew while she hands him his hoodie.

I say, "It'll be nice having her close."

"I think it'll do us all some good to have a friend here." Skylar pulls her hair into a high ponytail.

Drew says looking at me, "It nice that the two of you get along so well. I know she's Connor's mom, but I think she has a lot of respect for you."

Maybe because we've been through the same nightmare. "I have a lot of respect for her, too."

Rachael says, "You both have been through more than you should have. No one should have to live their life under those conditions. Not even for one minute."

She's right. No one should. We get the text that they're done and we should leave now to meet them at the bakery. I tuck the small gift I bought Nichole into my purse. It isn't much, just a little something to remind her how strong she is. When times get hard, I never want her to forget she's a fighter and she can do anything.

"You ready?" Drew asks.

"We are."

He drives us over to the bakery. The more I see of Savannah, the more I'm reminded that we've made the right decision to move here.

"I love this place," Skylar says, looking out the window at the busy streets and the manicured lawns.

"Me, too," Drew and I say simultaneously. It's nice to know that Drew likes it here, too. "It's a great area," I add.

When we pull up at the bakery, Chase and Nichole are already there. The blinds downstairs are up and the plantation shutters upstairs in the apartment are opened. Nothing says home like natural lighting. We walk in and Chase and Nichole are standing in the bakery.

"So, you got it?" I ask. I already know she does, but I have to hear her say it.

"I got it," she squeals, waving a fist full of papers in her hands. We all hug and it's a great feeling. She looks amazing and happy. Chase stands back and watches the interaction between everyone. "Now the real work begins."

She isn't kidding. It's hard work getting a business ready to open. "Yep, finding the perfect name is the hardest part of it all." *This is the best part, but I want to take her mind off of the real work that's ahead of her.*

"Oh, you're right. My bakery needs a name."

Skylar says, "It has to be something catchy, fun, and cute."

After several minutes of silence, she says, "Oh, Lord, this just might be the hardest part. Because right now, I have nothing."

"It's on a great street name. Maybe you can build on it," Rachael says.

"Magnolia Street is a beautiful name."

When no one says something, I say, "Here, I bought you a house-warming gift. It's not much, but it's something I found and thought of you."

Nichole hugs me and says, "Thank you, Ava." She opens it and reveals a picture frame. Inside the antique white frame is a saying: "Life isn't about finding yourself, it's about creating yourself." She cries. "Thank you, it's perfect. I have the perfect place for it." She walks over and sets it in the window sill. "Now I can see it everyday."

We toast Nichole and her fresh start. She cries and in turn, we all cry. It's a very emotional day. Rachael and Nichole have become good friends and I'm grateful for that.

"Shall we continue this party somewhere else?" Chase asks.

I look at Chase. "Where do you have in mind?"

"I made dinner reservations at Carla Jo Dean's. I'd say we better leave now to get there at the time I reserved."

I ride with Chase and he tells me how smoothly everything went today for Nichole. He doesn't say it, but I sense that he feared that maybe Brett could have caused problems for her. I know you don't need your attorney present to sign off on a property loan. I'm reminded again of what a great guy he is.

We have dinner and drinks and talk about the bakery. The more we drink, the more names we come up with for Nichole to consider. Chase suggests, "Magnolia, Meringue, and Muffins." We all laugh. Drew says, "I think 'Mincemeat and Macadamia Nuts on Magnolia Street' is a great name." I don't know if I should barf or plug my ears. When the food and the drinks are gone, we leave to go home.

Everyone is staying at the inn tonight and we all plan to go to the bakery tomorrow to clean. The furniture delivery will be arriving between 8:00 and 10:00 am. Chase opens the door first and we all shuffle in after him. "Here, this was on the doorstep." He hands me a box, wrapped in blue wrapping paper. It was hand delivered, not mailed.

"Oh, a secret admirer," Skylar teases.

I open the package as everyone watches. Inside the gift box is a set of two infant boy receiving blankets. I hear whispers before Rachael steps up and whispers, "Is there something you need to tell me?"

I look at her in confusion. "What?"

"You and Xander? Is there something I should know?"

What is she talking about? I look down the infant blankets. *Oh, shit! She thinks I'm pregnant.* "No. I'm not pregnant."

I look at Skylar for help. "Don't look at me, those were addressed to you."

Thanks a lot. First the positive pregnancy test, then these. "Someone's playing a joke on me." I explain about the pregnancy test I received earlier. "Some kids must be doing this as a prank."

Chase steps up and looks at the name on the package. "This isn't a child's handwriting."

I look at it and he's right. "I have no idea who sent this or why."

Rachael says, "Are you sure, Ava? Maybe it's a sign."

I take a deep breath. *Am I sure? We had protected sex. I don't have any symptoms of pregnancy. A sign? From whom? Xander? That's just crazy.* "I'm sure, Rachael. There's no way. Someone's just playing a joke on me." *Does she hope I'm pregnant with Xander's baby? Does she think if I am, a part of him will live on? It's sad and it makes me sad for her.*

Chase steps up and takes the pressure off me. "Well, there's no baby here, so let's get to bed so we can start bright and early on the 'Sweets Baked on Magnolia Street.'"

Everyone laughs at the new name he just gave Nichole's bakery. "We need to definitely work on a name," Nichole says. "Good night, everyone."

When everyone goes to bed, I toss the baby blankets into the bin of items we plan on donating to the Salvation Army. We started this bin when guests started leaving items behind in their rooms. Then I toss the gift box and wrapping paper into the trash.

Chase comes into the bedroom with me. "When did these pranks about a baby start?"

I sit on the bed and he sits at the foot. "I don't know, a few weeks ago."

"No idea who would do that?"

"None."

He stalls before saying, "I hate to ask, but is there any chance of a…"

"No." *I'm a little upset he would ask. I have been having dreams about babies and pregnancies. Could the baby I'm dreaming about be mine and Xander's? I feel sick. That's absurd to think that this could happen. I refuse to believe that.* "No, not at all."

"Okay. Just wanted to check." He stands and turns on the candles, the chirping birds CD, and the waterfall before leaving. "I'll see you in the morning. We have a big day."

"Good night."

"Sweet dreams."

Tonight, I don't dream of Connor, or beatings, or anger. I *do* dream of little cute babies who look like Xander. I wake in a cold sweat. My hearts races and I feel like I just saw into the future. There's no way. God, please, don't let this be a vision. I toss and turn and think about all of the unplanned pregnancies in this world because of faulty contraception. Please don't let this be one of them. I'm not ready to be a mom.

I turn off the chirping birds because this feels nothing like a paradise. I think of what would become of my life if I were pregnant. Xander's gone. I'd be a single mom trying to run a bed and breakfast. This wouldn't work. It couldn't work. Not with the hours I keep. I'm up at 4:30 am every day. Spending my Sundays baking and cooking for the week. *Where would a baby fit into this?*

Even if I were pregnant, the sender of the pregnancy test and the blankets wouldn't know. No one knew about my and Xander's intimate moments but us. Us and maybe Skylar. She wouldn't send me pranks like that. She knows it would make me worry.

With little sleep, I shower and put on a sweatshirt and yoga pants. I'm tired, but I'm ready to work. I'm ready to help to get Nichole's place in tip-top shape. This is a big day for her, and I'll do everything I can to be positive.

Since it's a bakery, Drew thought it was fitting to take breakfast there. "We'll have 'Donuts and Muffins on Magnolia,'" he teases, trying to incorporate a bakery name into his sentence. We do have donuts and muffins at the new bakery. The furniture comes and Rachael and Nichole instruct the delivery guys where everything goes, while everyone else continues cleaning. Drew and Chase are power washing the building, sidewalk, and the driveway, while Skylar and I continue cleaning and painting the inside.

Nichole and Rachael are excited about staying at the bakery tonight. They leave to go to the grocery store when we all leave to go home. On the way home, we stop by the store and I quickly and secretly buy a pregnancy test while everyone else is shopping. I shove it in my purse before joining the others. When Skylar, Chase, Drew, and I get home, a woman and a small child are sitting in the swing on the front porch of the inn.

We didn't have any reservations for tonight; maybe she's looking for a room at the last minute.

"Can I help you?" Skylar asks, getting out of the car.

"I'm looking for Ava." She stands, holding her small child.

I step around from the car and I immediately recognize the woman from Chase's office. *Lorraine.* She's blonde with big boobs, and she's very attractive. I look at her and then I look at her son. He looks familiar. I walk onto the large porch and Drew turns on the porch light. I stare at the boy. This isn't good. I get a bad feeling about this. He reminds me of someone. The hairs on my neck stand on end. Goosebumps cover my entire body.

"How can I help you?"

"Lorraine," Chase says curtly.

She doesn't acknowledge him. She stares me in the eye. Not blinking. "I came to get what is rightfully owed to my son."

I look at her son in confusion. I don't know her son; hell, I barely know her. "I'm confused. I'm sorry, but I don't know your son."

She takes a step closer to me. I can feel Skylar and Drew watching us. Chase takes a step closer.

"Lorraine?" Chase says sternly.

"Does he look familiar to you, Ava? Take a good long look at him. Does he remind you of anyone?"

I look away from Lorraine and focus my attention on her son. He looks so familiar. He looks like every baby picture I ever saw of Connor. It can't be. Connor and I were married for two years. He's been dead for over a year.

"How, how old is your son?" I stutter.

"He's almost two." She smiles and it's almost sinister.

I look even more closely at the dark-haired boy. I feel faint. I feel sick. Holding onto the porch railing for support, I say, "He's Connor's."

"He is, he looks like just like his daddy, don't you think?"

Chase

I always thought Lorraine was a bit crazy, but now I'm sure of it. I look at her baby and I think he looks like any other child his age. I don't see any resemblance to Connor, Brett, or Nichole whatsoever. "What are you talking about?"

"Chase, butt out. This has nothing to do with you. This has to do with me, little Connor, Ava, and my son's inheritance that he didn't get when his father died."

Bitch, if Ava's involved then I have everything to do with this. "You didn't get anything from Connor because you weren't entitled to anything." I take a step forward and whisper so only she can hear me. "If I were you, I would take your crazy ass home, and get some help."

Ava speaks and her voice is a near whisper. "How am I to believe that your son belongs to Connor?"

Lorraine pulls paperwork from her overstuffed handbag. "Because DNA doesn't lie."

She doesn't offer it to Ava, and I'm not sure that I believe she's actually holding proof. *I knew she and Connor were close, but did I think they were this close? Perhaps I suspected it a time or two.* "Why are you coming forward now? Why not come forward right after Connor's death?"

Lorraine laughs as she readjusts her son on her hip. "Chase, you know how this works. You hire an attorney, they want proof, Family and Children Services want proof, the Social Security Administration wants proof, the judge wants proof. The list is endless. No one can just take your word that the child is his."

Ava looks at me and I fear that she may think I know something about this. "Well, we want proof, too."

Lorraine looks at Ava and smiles as she walks in between us. "Oh, you'll get it. My attorney will be in touch. I just wanted to give you a heads up so you'll be prepared. I just hate surprises, don't you?" she says as she walks off the porch to her car.

"Why, that bitch," Skylar says as she starts to walk off the porch after Lorraine.

Drew reaches out and grabs her by the arm. "Oh, no, you don't, Killer."

Skylar stands tall and says, "If you think I'm going to sit back and let this happen to my best friend, then you're crazier than that crazy bitch."

"Come on, Skylar, she isn't worth it," Ava walks into the house and we follow behind her. She walks into the kitchen and pours herself a glass of wine. She downs half the glass and says, "Chase, do you know if Connor was having an affair on me?"

"No, Ava, I don't." I look her in the eye so she can see my sincerity.

"You worked with them, you didn't suspect anything?"

My mind replays the years that Connor and I worked together. I was so focused on making partner of the law firm that if they had sex on the desk in front of me, I'm not sure I would have noticed. I did hear a rumor or two about them, but I didn't believe that Connor would stray away from Ava for something like Lorraine. "I didn't."

Ava refills her glass with wine and sits down. Skylar grabs three wine glasses and the bottle and follows Ava into the living room. I want to say something but I'm speechless. I have no idea what to say. I see Ava hurting and I hate seeing her like this.

"You don't believe that crazy bitch, do you?" Skylar says, pouring Drew, me, and herself a glass.

"Did you look at that baby?"

Skylar says. "I did. He was cute. He looked nothing like that ugly ass you were married to."

"Skylar, he looked just like every baby picture I ever saw of Connor." Ava holds her stomach and says, "I'm gonna be sick." She stands and runs into the bathroom.

"I'll attend to her," Skylar says. "You guys, go and see if Nichole knows anything about this."

Why didn't I think about that? "We'll be back."

On the drive to Nichole's, I fill Drew in on the piece-of-shit guy that Ava was married to. I'm sure that Skylar's told him some things, but he may be hearing more than he expected to once we get to Nichole's. I have no idea if Lorraine is hallucinating or what her evil plot is, but I don't like it. I call Nichole and let her know that we're coming over. I hate to ruin her housewarming, but she may be the one person who holds the answers.

Nichole and Rachael are up decorating the apartment when we get there. I feel bad because she has no idea of the bomb I'm about to drop.

"What brings you boys out this time of night?" Nichole asks.

There's no easy way to say it, so I just come right out with it. "When we got home this evening, Lorraine Williams was at the inn waiting on Ava." I watch as the name sinks in. *Nothing.* "Do you remember her? She was Connor's secretary."

Nichole shifts on her seat. "What did she want?"

"She had her son with her and she's claiming that her son, Connor, belongs to your son, Connor." I continue. "As you can imagine, Ava's pretty upset." When she doesn't say anything, I ask, "Do you know anything about this?"

She sits up on the edge of the couch. "No, this is all new to me. I think I met her once or twice and one of those times was at Connor's funeral." I'm relieved when she says she doesn't know anything about Lorraine or her baby. I didn't want to think that she was capable of deceiving Ava, especially after everything that Ava's been through and has done to help her in these recent weeks.

"Wait a minute," she says. "I vaguely remember something that happened with Lorraine."

I watch as she searches her memory. "What was it?"

"It was after Connor's death. Marshall and Brett went to clean out Connor's desk."

"I remember that day, Lorraine was there helping. I think I had court or something and couldn't stay."

"A few days later I heard Brett talking on the phone. He was in his office and he didn't want me to hear. He said to whoever he was talking to that he found something in Connor's desk."

"What was it?"

"That part I couldn't hear. But I thought he was talking to Marshall."

Would Ava's dad keep a secret from her, especially something like this? How far would a father go to protect his daughter?

Ava

When Drew and Chase leave, I have a meltdown in front of Skylar. I don't know why, even I don't understand it. The way Connor treated me throughout our marriage, why would I care if he had an affair on me? Why would that even bother me? I have no idea, but it does. *Infidelity is different. The beatings I suffered at the hands of Connor, although I have no memory of them, at times I wonder if maybe I didn't deserve them. Could I have provoked them? Did I deserve them in some sick way? But an affair? That's different. To have an affair during our marriage… and to conceive a child? I can't begin to explain to Skylar how that feels. I feel betrayed. I feel like I wasn't good enough. I feel sick knowing my husband was with another woman intimately.*

"If he was that unhappy with me, then why wouldn't he just leave me? Why stay with someone if you're totally and completely miserable?"

"Ava, I wish I knew. I wish I had the answers. Connor wasn't right. If he was, he never would have been the kind of husband he was to you. This isn't about you and you not being good enough. It's about Connor and his problems that made him behave the way he did." She drinks more wine. "Besides, we don't even know if that *is* Connor's baby. She probably stole that kid from Walmart, brought him here, and is trying to pass him off as her own. There's probably an Amber alert right now and police are looking for him."

I want to laugh, but I can't. I wipe the steady flow of tears, hating the way I'm thinking and feeling right now. Connor was an ass. Why do I even care what he and Lorraine did? He's gone.

"What do you think her purpose was for coming over here?"

"She said she wanted money. The inheritance from Connor."

I replay her words over and over in my head: "I came to get what is rightfully owed to my son. I came to get what is rightfully owed to my son. I came to get what is rightfully owed to my son." I say, "Skylar? If that baby is Connor's, is she entitled to half of everything?"

"I have no idea. Chase would know more than I would." She watches me and I can see when she realizes my concern. "You bought this house with Connor's money."

"I did. I sold our family home. There's money in the bank, in IRA's…" I take a deep breath before I finish. "If she's entitled to half…"

"Let's think about this. If the kid is Connor's and he was alive, she would get child support."

"Right." I down my wine and pour another glass. "But he's not alive, so they would get something from Social Security, right?"

"A monthly check."

"Right. But would they get half of everything? Like in a divorce?"

"Ava, I think you need to call your mom and dad. They need to know what's going on."

"Good idea." Feeling more tipsy than I felt a few moments ago. I stand to get my phone from my purse. Swaying, I try to focus in on my contacts. I call Dad, hoping he'll answer his phone first. He does. I tell him what happened, and before I can finish he says, "We're on our way." I disconnect the call and stumble to the couch.

"What did he say?"

Skylar holds up the nearly empty wine bottle and offers me some. I shake my head. I've had enough. "They're on the way." I look at the clock trying to focus in on the blurred numbers. "Is that 11:00?" Before she can answer I say, "I'm drunk."

She also squints her eyes while looking at the clock. "Do we have guests?" She blinks fast. "Do we have to get up in the morning?"

"Nope. The house is empty." I say with more slurring than I expected. "I'm drunk and I'm going to bed."

"Me, too."

In the morning I feel no better than I did when I went to bed. My stomach hurts, my head hurts, and my vision's blurry. I remember last night and the visit with Lorraine. I remember wine, lots and lots of wine. I also remember I went to bed before Chase, Mom, and Dad got here. When I finally decide to open my eyes, Skylar is in bed with me. It's a big bed and I didn't even know she was there.

Running to the bathroom, I throw up the remaining stomach contents of my drunken night. If this is a sample of how my day's going to be, I'm not impressed or excited to start my morning. Knowing I should shower, I decide coffee and Tylenol should be first on my agenda. No sooner than I leave the bathroom, Skylar runs in. I hear her dry heaving and I decide I should leave the room before I start again. I can already see the bathroom being a revolving door — the thought makes my head spin.

Drew and Chase are already up having coffee when I walk out into the living room. Chase's blankets are folded and sitting on one end of the couch. I see three empty wine bottles still on the coffee table. Deciding they can wait, I head for the coffee pot.

"Is that my girlfriend I hear?" Drew asks.

I sure hope so. If not, it means I spent the night with a total stranger. "She might need something for a headache." I search the cabinet for any bottle with the phrase "pain relief" written on it. *I'm still not sure why or how Skylar ended up in my bed. She's like a sister so I'm not too worried.*

"A headache or a hangover?" he asks.

Licking my dry lips I say, "Same difference." I take two Tylenol tablets and give the bottle to Drew. I down them with a glass of water. I can see Chase watching me as I make my way to the coffee pot.

"Do you know if my mom and dad are here?" I ask without looking at him.

"They are. I think they got here about 3:00."

"Coffee?" I ask, holding up the pot.

"I'm good."

I have a million things I want to ask him, but I can't form a coherent thought right now. I sit across from him, cup the hot mug around my hands, and inhale. I just need to sit and collect my thoughts. I need to think about what happened last night. God, I wish I hadn't drunk so much. The alcohol clouds my thoughts and impairs my judgment. At times, I like that feeling, but not today, not now. I need to have a clear head so I can figure this all out. I'm grateful when Mom and Dad aren't up.

Skylar walks out of the bedroom looking like death. Drew helps her from my bedroom into hers. "Shower" is the only word that passes through his lips. She doesn't say anything but walks slowly beside him.

When I finish my first cup of coffee, Mom and Dad walk through the living quarters. I greet them both with a kiss and a hug.

"I'm glad to see you, Chase. Let me get a coffee, then I'll be ready to start," Dad says, walking to the coffee pot.

"I need a shower. I really, really need a shower."

While showering, I think about my life being an open book. I'm sure if this happened to anyone else, the problem with Lorraine would have been kept very private. Who wants to flash their dysfunctional life for everyone to see? My amnesia's to blame. I have no secrets from anyone. The secrets I do have, I can't remember. I've been fine living my life in only the present. I need to remember my past. I need to focus more on trying to remember the first 25 years of my life. If I could remember my past, maybe I wouldn't have been so shocked when Lorraine told me my husband fathered her child. Maybe I knew about the affair. Maybe I knew he was seeing someone else and that's when the beatings started.

Instead of sinking into a depression that threatens me, I'm determined to get the answers I need and want. I get dressed with a newfound determination. I need to remember. I need to find a way to remember my past, no matter how brutal it is. I need to research ways for me to jog my memory. Not the lame way I tried in the past. No more visiting places I've been to. No more searching old photos. I need something more extreme. I have an idea.

First, I need to see if Lorraine's son is really Connor's and if he stands to inherit half of what I own. If he does, I may be in trouble financially. I paid cash for the bed and breakfast with Skylar repaying me in payments. The inn does okay, but it's not a goldmine by any means. I have money in saving and investments, but if I have to share my money, I won't have the cushion I'm used to. *Will the income from the inn give me enough money to make it, or would I be forced to sell the inn? What would Skylar do? She quit her job to move here with me. What would I do? Go back to work as a nurse. Would anyone hire me with amnesia? Would I be a liability to them?* Yes, I would be. If something went terribly wrong, I could say, "I have amnesia, I couldn't remember what I was supposed to do." Of course, I would never say or do that, but an employer might think it could happen.

Drew and Skylar leave and gives us some alone time. Although my life is open for all, it's embarrassing and I don't want everyone knowing every dirty detail. Of course, I'll fill Skylar in on everything when they return. She's my best friend and she knows more about me than I do about myself. Chase, Mom, Dad, and I sit around the dining room table while I tell Mom and Dad exactly what happened when we returned home last night. They both look sad at what I tell them. Mom brings up a valid point. "Where would she get Connor's DNA to prove that her son was his?"

My eyes get big with the possibility that maybe this won't be true. It's my first sign of hope. "I never thought of that."

Mom look around the table. "They couldn't exhume his body without Ava's permission."

"No one contacted me about doing such a thing. Could Brett and Nichole give permission?" I ask. "They are his parents."

"No, he was married," Chase says, "They would go through you first, then if they didn't get the answers they wanted, they would try to get permission from his next of kin. Which after you, it's them. Not unless... but that's highly unlikely."

What's highly unlikely? "What is?" *I want to yell it but I remain calm.*

"Lorraine and Connor had a DNA test done prior to his death."

Why would he do that?

Dad just listens. Mom says, "But she was pregnant when Connor died. Would they do it while the baby is in utero?"

"They could." Chase looks away from me and looks at Dad. "If Connor believed in all likelihood the baby could be his, I could see him agreeing to have the DNA test done prior to delivery."

I think I'm going to be sick.

Dad watches Chase. "But if she had proof in that paper she was waving around she got from her purse, why wouldn't she just show it to Ava then?"

Yay, this gives me hope. I start to open my mouth and Chase says, "I think she's bluffing."

Do I dare hope this is a plot to extort money from me and this will all pass over? "Stop," I say, covering my ears. "This is too much. It sounds like something I would watch on television." I want to cry while thinking about all that is happening. "I can't take anymore right now." Mom pats my hand. "I can't change the past, but I also don't want to live in limbo. Is there anyway we can find out who her attorney is, if there even is an attorney, and start moving forward to finding out the truth?"

"I'm sorry, Ava. I can do what I can. I can ask around and see what the other attorneys are saying. Maybe they've heard something."

"Thank you. I'm scared if she'll get half, then I might have to sell the inn. If I do, I have no idea what I'll do."

Skylar

I went to sleep in my own bed last night until Ava woke up screaming about a baby. I went to her room and I could barely get her to stop sobbing. Drew and Chase weren't home yet, so I decided to just crawl in bed with her and sleep. I thought maybe being near her would keep her demons at bay.

After I shower and sober up, I tell Ava that Drew and I are heading out to spend some time down by Tybee Island. It was a lie. I'm a friend on a mission and thankfully, my boyfriend is on board with it.

He drove as I searched every hotel, motel, and bed and breakfast in the Savannah area. We start at the inn and then circle around it, checking places as we make bigger and bigger circles, looking for the yellow sports car that Lorraine was driving last night. When we can't find her, Drew and I decide to drive over to Nichole's place. I like her and I know she's been through a lot, but so help me, if she knows something about that raggedy-ass-son of hers, I don't know what I'll do.

I know Connor is her son and she has that unconditional love I always read about in books, but really, can you love someone like that, even if he is your son? Yes, I guess you can. You just don't love what they do. I get that. She can love him, but she better not be keeping anything from Ava. *Would a married man confide in his parents that he may have fathered a child with another woman?* I think about this carefully. Connor wouldn't confide in Nichole, but that snake-in-the- grass *would* confide in his slimy-ass father.

"Let's go home. Nichole doesn't know anything."

"Wait? What? How do you know? Maybe she remembered something since last night." Drew watches the road, glancing over at me only once.

"Connor wouldn't have confided in his mother. She would have frowned upon his actions. That piece of shit of a so-called man probably confided in his piece-of-shit father."

Drew doesn't turn onto Magnolia Street; he bypasses it and heads to the inn. "If his dad is anything like I hear Ava's ex-husband is, his father might have looked at this situation proudly."

I get sick to my stomach, thinking of those two laughing and toasting their brandy to such hideous news. "If this isn't some hoax, then I'm sure Brett knows all about it. He probably even hired Lorraine an attorney."

Drew smiles a wicked smile. "Shouldn't be hard to find out who her attorney is."

Sweet baby Jesus, my man's not only hot, sexy, and good in bed, but he's also a genius. When we pull up at the house, everyone but Ava is sitting in the tearoom. Claire tells me that Ava's napping. I run through what Drew and I talked about and how we think Brett might be behind this. We tell them everything that we talked about and it's likely that

Lorraine didn't have money for counsel so Brett might have hired an attorney for her.

Ava walks in behind me. "So you think the baby is Connor's?"

Shit, I didn't want her to hear any of this. "No, I never said that."

"I heard what you said. You think that Brett hired an attorney for her."

I look at her sympathetically. She looks like she's been crying. "Ava, I honestly have no idea. But what I do know is that Brett is just as slimy as Connor. Maybe this is all made up. Maybe Lorraine's looking for a quick payday. Maybe this is Brett's way of getting back at you and Nichole." *I think for a minute and that doesn't make sense.* "Is this an example of the twisted way of how he thinks? I don't know. But if this is for real, then yes, I would say that Brett is well aware and he would have hired his own shady attorney." *I have no idea if their attorney is shady, but in my experience, the sleaze on people like this makes them stick together.*

"Why would he do that?" Ava sits down at an empty chair. "What does he have to gain from any of this?"

I don't know. I have to think for a minute before it clicks. "He lost his only son. Maybe he wants a boy in the family to carry on his 'legacy,'" I say, using air quotes. *I personally would like to see his legacy die and never be rebirthed.* "I have no idea what twisted people think about."

Chase says, "I think you're right about Brett and possibly hiring his attorney or one who is known to him." He looks at Ava sadly. "We can sit and wait it out to see if this is a bluff, or go at it proactively and look for our own answers."

"I think that's a good idea. I need to know as soon as I can." Ava stands and turns to face everyone. "There's something else." I watch Ava closely as she wrings her hands together in a nervous gesture. "I know that my past is one that should be forgotten. Some days, I wake up and I'm grateful that I can't remember anything about it." Her voice trails off. "Then I'm faced with something like this and I try so hard to remember. I don't like people knowing things about my life that I should know. I don't like the surprises that come knocking at my door, and I don't like the nightmares that haunt me and steal my sleep almost every night." A tear falls. "I've been thinking about this and I want to remember. I need to remember. No matter how bad it was, I need to remember so I can move on to a future."

"Ava?" Claire says sweetly. "How do you plan to do this? You can't just decide one day you're going to remember and your memory comes back to you."

"That's where my family is going to come into play." *I'm confused.* "I suspect that my family and some of my friends, not you, Drew," she teases, "are keeping something from me. I don't think you do it out of meanness, I think you're doing it to protect me."

"Ava, I swear I didn't know what Connor was doing to you. I would have stopped him. I would have killed that bastard myself," I say. *She can't think that her family and friends would have stood by and done nothing.*

"Not things to that extent. Skylar, I know you would have done everything in your power to help me. I don't ever question that. But sometimes I think that you guys know things and hide them from me. I'm strong and I can take whatever it is you're afraid to tell me. I think if you quit trying so hard to protect me, maybe I'll be better off in the long run."

I think about what she says and the only secret I know about Ava is that Chase is in love with her. My eyes quickly dart toward him. He watches me and shakes his head slightly. I quickly look away. This is his secret and if he wants to tell her, then I'll support that. I'm not exactly sure how that'll jog her memory. I also see Marshall looking at Chase. Does Marshall know what I know? Chase looks away and watches Ava. I now suspect that something is up between those two. What secrets are those two keeping? I don't know, but I intend to find out. I don't have anything to say. I guess in a sense, I'm keeping something from her. If I say I'm not, it'll be a lie.

Claire says, "Ava, I've told you everything I know." *Of course she has. She's her mother, she wouldn't keep anything from her daughter.*

Ava

I look at each person and other than Mom and Drew, I swear they all look guilty of something. Mom was the only one who said she wasn't keeping something from me and I believe her. Chase, Skylar, and even my dad sat there and said nothing. I would be lying if I said that didn't hurt. "Well, if anyone has something to tell me that might help me to get my memory back, I'll be in my room." I turn to leave and then look back and say, "Chase, whatever you can find out about Lorraine and her lawyer, if she has one, will you keep me posted?"

He looks at Dad before answering. "I will."

I don't smile. I can't. I feel deceived. "Thank you."

I just announced to everyone that I was strong enough to hear the truth, yet I feel like I want to cry all the way to my room. I lie on the bed with my door slightly cracked. I think of Xander. I miss him. *If he knew what a mess I was, would he have left and never turned back? How was he so strong?*

He was strong up until the day of his surgery. I never saw him when he didn't look in total control. Does he know my problems? Can he see everything that's unfolding in front of me? Maybe he can help me?

There's a knock at the door and it's Chase. He watches me as he walks in. "Hey, you don't need to knock." I sit up in the bed and he sits on the edge. Chase has known me a long time. Surely he knows something about my life, about my past, that could trigger a memory.

I just want to lie in his arms and have him hold me. I just want for him to take away all this bad stuff so I can try to pick up my broken life and move toward a better future. He doesn't say anything but opens his hands palm side up. I smile and place my hands in his. They're warm and inviting. I get this familiar feeling that we've held hands before.

"Ava," he says in a low raspy voice. "I've been keeping something from you." He closes his hands and they engulf mine.

I knew it. He knows something. I don't know whether to be mad or thrilled. I brace myself for the worst. "What is it?"

He releases my hold and runs his hand through his thick hair. "I... I'm..." He clears his throat and pins me with his gaze. "I don't know how to tell you this."

"Please. Chase. It's me. You can tell me anything."

"Not this, Ava. You won't understand. I wanted to tell you. I should have told you sooner. But... I couldn't find the words. Skylar told me you should know."

"Skylar? What does Skylar have to do with this?"

He searches for eyes. "God, Ava. I don't want you to be mad."

"Chase, you're frightening me. Just tell me."

I try to hold eye contact, but Chase looks away. He releases my hand and stands. "I can't. I can't do this. Not now. I'm sorry."

He starts to walk to the door. I chase after him and block the exit so he can't leave. Whatever he has to tell me, I need to hear it. I need for him to just say it. Tears fill my eyes and spill over.

"I need to know. I need to remember my past. Please, if you know something, you need to tell me. I'm begging you, please." I'll get on my hands and knees if I need to. I'll beg and plead and cry. I'll do whatever I need to make him tell me.

He cups my face and wipes away my tears. He searches my eyes with his sad ones. "Don't cry." I can't help it. Every time I blink, tears falls. "You're so beautiful." He knows something that could help restore my memory. Am I ready for this? Am I prepared to remember things that my mind blocked out? I am. I need to be. I can't move forward to a future if I can't leave the past.

"Ava, this will change everything. Everything that you knew to be the truth, will all be a lie."

Oh, God. This is bad. My hands are sweaty, my heart's racing, and my knees are wobbly. I feel sick. Be strong, Ava. "I need to know. I can handle this, Chase." I hope I can. I hope I'm ready for whatever he has to tell me.

"I hope you're ready for this." Still cupping my face, he says, "I love you. I loved you in college. I loved you when you married Connor, and I still love you. I think I loved you the moment I first saw you."

He leans in and kisses me, and I kiss him back. Sweetly. Softly. Passionately. He places his hand on the small of my back and brings me to him. "I love you, too," I whisper.

There's a knock at the door and I wonder who could be knocking. Not now. Go away. Chase continues to kiss me. I let him. My lips feel numb from the passion. It's a great feeling. I want more. I want Chase.

"Ava? Can I come in?"

The voice is familiar. No, go away. I don't want to be bothered. I breathe heavily as Chase walks me toward the bed. "I want you," he rasps.

"I want you, too."

"Ava, it's Chase. Can I come in?"

Wait? What? I'm kissing Chase. How can Chase be at the door knocking?

"I want you. I wanted to tell you, but I was afraid. I was afraid you wouldn't feel the same way about me. God, I love you, Ava."

"Ava, it's Chase. Are you awake?"

With my eyes still closed. I try to calm my heavy breathing. My lips still swollen from the kiss. My face red from the blush. My heart racing with excitement. A dream. It was all a dream. Another knock at the door.

"Ava, I'm coming in."

Chase

When Ava doesn't answer, I open her bedroom door slowly. She's in bed sound asleep. It's not like her to sleep so long during the day. I want to go to her, but I close the door and let her sleep instead. Skylar said Ava has nightmares nightly. This must be exhausting for her. I hate that she dreams of Connor, and her past that she can't remember. Although Ava can't see it, I know that since her dreams are memories, then her amnesia is a blessing. God is protecting her from an unimaginable past. She made a desperate plea just hours before for us to tell her things that may help her remember. Skylar told me it's time I tell Ava my true feelings. It's time for me to open up about how I truly feel for her. I can't. I can't risk that Ava won't reciprocate back. What if Ava wants nothing to do with me once I tell her? I can't risk losing her. I'd rather have her in my life as a friend than not have her in my life at all.

Ava

I pretend to sleep until Chase leaves. I force myself to take shallow breaths. I can't let him see me like this. My dreams and nightmares have always been about violence and hatred, that is, up until now. *What in the hell was that?* This dream was just moments shy of being a wet dream. *Do I have those kinds of feelings for him? I certainly did in my dream. I touch my tingling lips. Have I ever been kissed like that? It was sexy and sensual. Have I ever wanted anyone as much as I wanted Chase? Great! Just something else to add to my already confused mind.*

I get up and shower as I try to make sense of this. It'll give me some time to get my breathing under control. It's too much. It's too much to add on top of everything else. Maybe I was dreaming of Xander. *No, that was definitely not Xander in my dream. Chase? Will I ever be able to look at him the same?*

I slip into a long-sleeved white-tee and a pair of jeans before joining my family in the living room. Chase, Drew, and Dad are gone and I'm a bit relieved. I'm not ready to see Chase so soon after *that* dream. Mom and Skylar are watching a rerun of *Friends*.

"Where's the guys?"

"They went to Staples," Skylar says. "You slept a long time. Do you feel better?"

"I do. Do you guys want to go see Nichole? I'd like to see how her place is coming along."

Mom says, "I'd love to."

"Me, too," Skylar says, standing.

During the drive to Nichole's bakery, I text her to make sure it's okay that we come over. I also order take-out and call Dad and tell him that's where we'll be. We pull into the parking lot and I take a deep breath. Mom and Skylar didn't talk about Lorraine, Connor, or anything unpleasant on the ride here. I hope that Nichole and Rachael don't mention it either. I can't forget about it, but I also don't want it to be the main topic of every conversation either. There's nothing I can do about it, so I'll just wait and see what happens. It sure has done nothing for my self-esteem.

I put on a smile as we carry take-out Chinese food upstairs to Nichole's new apartment. I'm happy to see that the outside entrance looks inviting. Since I was here yesterday, Nichole added a winter wreath on the door and a couple small wooden rockers beside the newly painted "haint blue" color door. I smile as I remember the story of this color being used to keep the spirits out of your home. *Maybe I need to paint my bedroom door this color.*

The door opens before we have a chance to knock. Nichole greets us warmly as Rachael stands close by. We make pleasantries before we set the food out on the dining room table.

"This place looks amazing," I say truthfully.

Drew, Chase, and Dad arrive just before dinner. I'm nervous about seeing Chase. My hands get sweaty and I'm not sure how to act. Do I act like I'm glad to see him? Do I ignore him? Do I greet him with a hug? How did I act toward him before the dream? I can't remember. I decide it's best to just stay put and attend to the food. When I hear his voice, my face flushes red.

"What's wrong with you?" Skylar asks.

"Nothing. Why?" I ask, placing the serving spoons in the General Tso Chicken and Shrimp Lo Mein.

"You're all flushed. Are you getting sick?"

Sick! Why didn't I think of that? "I don't feel well."

"Who's sick?" Dad asks.

"Ava. She's all flushed and sweaty."

Thanks, Skylar. I look up through thick lashes and everyone is looking at me. "I'm sure it's nothing. There's just a lot going on." At least that part is the truth.

"When did this start?" Mom asks.

Just since I had a near wet dream about Chase. "Shortly after I woke up," I say instead. Chase looks concerned as he walks toward me. "I'm going to the restroom and splash some water on my face. It's hot in here," I lie. "I'll be back in a few minutes." *I need to get away. I can't talk to him right now. I pick up my purse and head to the nearest restroom.*

Closing the door tightly behind me, I lean against it. After several deep breaths, I look in the mirror. I look like a mess. *Get it together, Ava.* Reaching into my purse for my compact, I pull out a sack. It's the pregnancy test I bought yesterday. I sit on the toilet before I fall down. My time with Xander runs through my mind. The things we said, the places we went, and the few times we made love. My heart hurts that he isn't here. *Can I be pregnant?* I have been pretty nauseous lately. *Well, there's only one way to find out.* I read the directions and decide there's no better time like the present. I pee on the stick and wait... and wait... and wait. When I hear Chase tell Skylar in the other room to check on me, I decide I don't have time to wait for the result. Shoving the box, the pregnancy test strip, and the instructions into my purse, I join my family and friends.

Books By Brenda Kennedy

I support Indie Authors. If you read this book, please take the time to go to the purchasing site and give it a review.

Independent authors count on your reviews to get the word out about our books. Thank you for taking the time to read my books and taking the extra time to review them. I appreciate it very much.

Disclaimer: People and places in this book have been used fictitiously and without malice.

The Forgotten Trilogy

Book One: Leaving the Past

Book Two: Living for Today

Book Three: Seeking the Future …**Coming soon**

Other books written by this author include:

The Starting Over Trilogy

Book One: A New Beginning

Book Two: Saving Angel

Book Three: Destined to Love

The Freedom Trilogy

Book One: Shattered Dreams

Book Two: Broken Lives

Book Three: Mending Hearts

The Fighting to Survive Trilogy

Round One: A Life Worth Fighting

Round Two: Against the Odds

Round Three: One Last Fight

The Rose Farm Trilogy

Book One: Forever Country

Book Two: Country Life

Book Three: Country Love

Stand-alone books in the "Another Round of Laughter Series" written by Brenda and some of her siblings: Carla Evans, Martha Farmer, Rosa Jones, and David Bruce

Cupcakes Are Not A Diet Food …**Now available**

Kids Are Not Always Angels …**Coming soon**

Acknowledgements

My husband, Rex: Thank you for supporting me and for coming with me on this ride. Thank you for understanding that although I am in my pajamas, I am indeed working. You are my partner for life, and I love you.

My children: Thank you for reminding me what is important every single day. I love you.

My grandchildren: Thank you for reminding me that I am somebody; I am your grandma and nothing else matters. I love you all.

My sisters and brothers: Thank you for your endless support. I love you.

My brother David: Without you, I wouldn't have been able to publish the first book. Thank you for making my ideas better and for all you do. Editing, proofreading, polishing, formatting, ideas, articles, and research websites. See, I do pay attention. Thank you. Thank you for pushing me until I get it right. Maybe someday I'll learn the right place to put the commas. I love you and I can never thank you enough. I love you. David writes collections of anecdotes such as *The Funniest People in Art*, and he retells classics in such books as *William Shakespeare's* The Taming of the Shrew: *A Retelling in Prose*. His books can be found for sale on all leading online electronic book sale platforms.

Christina Badder, Owner and Operator of CBB Productions: My P.A., and my friend. Thank you for taking care of all of my promotional needs. The blog tours, author spotlights, book cover reveals, give-a-ways, Rafflecopters, ARC's, and everything that I don't know that you do or things I forgot to mention. I hope you know how much I appreciate your hard work and dedication. Girl, I love your work and your vision. You are so amazing and I am so glad I found you. I plan on keeping you, forever. For more info on Christina and her amazing work, see www.cbbproductions.com. Christina is also a LuLaRoe consultant, if you're looking to purchase the softest leggings around.

Becki Angle Martin: Thank you for designing this stunning cover. You saw my vision and brought it to life. Thank you.

Thank you to all of my Beta readers: You are amazing and I couldn't do it without you. I appreciate your honest opinions and reviews, and I love the bond that we have developed. Also, I appreciate that I can trust you and count on you. Thank you for encouraging me to write and for giving me ideas. You never disappoint. I love you guys!

Thank you to "Brenda's Street Talkers" for sharing my books, making teasers and banners, and for the love and support I receive from you every day. I love you girls.

Thank you to all the bloggers who shared in the author's spotlight and the blog tour for *Forgetting the Past*. I appreciate you more than you know.

A very special thank you to author DB Jones for your endless and continuous support. I feel like I've known you my entire life.

To my readers: Thank you for reading and reviewing my books. Thank you to my loyal readers who have followed me from the beginning and to those who are new to my books.

For those readers who enjoy a darker, more intense read: My daughter Carleen Jamison has recently published her debut novel, titled *Inappropriate Reactions*. It is Book One of the Mind Games Series. This book is intended for mature audiences only and is available on all leading platforms. You can follow her on

Smashwords Author's page:
https://www.smashwords.com/profile/view/carleenjamison

Facebook Author's Page:
https://www.facebook.com/author.c.jamison?fref=ts

Info for David Bruce, My Brother

Smashwords (Books for Sale, and Free Books)

http://www.smashwords.com/profile/view/bruceb

WordPress Blog

https://davidbruceblog.wordpress.com

About the Author

When I first started writing, I wanted to write about real people whom others could relate to with real-life problems and real jobs. I love to read about the billionaire 20-something-year-old, but knew this wasn't the kind of story I want to write. When my first trilogy, *The Starting Over Trilogy*, took form, I was thrilled to be able to make the book as close to realistic as I could.

I wanted to touch on real-life problems. Not because I want to show the weakness in my characters or to show the disturbing truth, but because I want to show my characters' strengths. *The Starting Over Trilogy* dealt with domestic violence: a problem that is all too familiar to too many women and men.

Next came *The Freedom Trilogy*, a spinoff of *The Starting Over Trilogy*. The series started off with the All-American military family and the real problems some face during deployment. I picked my daughter Amanda's brain and used her real emotions during the deployment stage. Thank you, Amanda. Then the story turned to drug abuse and rehabilitation.

The Fighting to Survive Trilogy focuses on battles of a boxer, depression, and how to move forward after the loss of a child. It tells the story of two families who are fighting the same battle.

Then *The Rose Farm Trilogy* took form. This series takes place in my old hometown in rural Ohio. I was excited to revisit my country roots and quickly learned that although I now live in Florida, I was never far from home. This series focuses on poverty in rural areas and how little a person needs to be truly happy. Although it takes place in my old hometown, the people and the circumstances are purely fictional, except for Rick Crooks and his sister.

I hope that in my future books I am still able to continue to write about problems most of us face while continuing to give my characters the happily ever after that they deserve. On a lighter note: I moved to sunny Florida in 2006 and never looked back. I love freshly squeezed lemonade, crushed ice, teacups, wine glasses, non-franchise restaurants, ice cream cones, boating, picnics, cookouts, throwing parties, lace, white wine, mojitos, strawberry margaritas, white linen tablecloths, fresh flowers, lace, mountains, oceans, and Pinterest. I also love to read and write and to spend time with my family.

My books, thus far, have been inspired by the things I love and the people who influence me, every single day, to be a better person.

You may follow me on:

FB author page : http://on.fb.me/1ywRwmI

BookBub Author's Page:
https://www.bookbub.com/authors/brenda-kennedy

GoodReads : http://bit.ly/1szWiw5

Twitter : https://twitter.com/BrendaKennedy_

Webpage: http://brendakennedyauthor.com

42577999R00141

Made in the USA
Middletown, DE
15 April 2017